Moon Over the Mountain

a quilting cozy

Carol Dean Jones

C&T PUBLISHING

Library of Congress Cataloging-in-
Publication Data

Names: Jones, Carol Dean, author.

Title: Moon over the mountain : a
quilting cozy / Carol Dean Jones.

Description: Lafayette, California :
C&T Publishing, [2018] | Series:
Quilting cozy series ; book 6

Identifiers: LCCN 2018003621 |
ISBN 9781617457425 (softcover)

Subjects: LCSH: Quilting--Fiction.
| Retirees--Fiction. | Retirement
communities--Fiction. | GSAFD:
Mystery fiction.

Classification: LCC PS3610.O6224 M66
2018 | DDC 813/.6--dc23

LC record available at
https://lccn.loc.gov/2018003621

A Quilting Cozy Series

by Carol Dean Jones

Acknowledgments

My sincere appreciation goes out to
my special friends Phyllis Inscoe,
Janice Packard, Sharon Rose,
and Barbara Small.

I thank each of you for the many hours
you have spent reading these chapters,
for bringing plot inconsistencies
and errors to my attention, and for
your endless encouragement.

I would like to offer special
appreciation to Joyce Marlane Frazier
who has tirelessly combed through
this manuscript and the entire
series looking for those pesky errors
that evade the author's eye.

Thank you, dear friends, for all your
hard work and for bringing fun to
what could otherwise have been
a tedious endeavor.

Chapter 1

"Another retreat?" Sophie asked. "Is this one on a boat?"
"It was a ship, Sophie, not a boat. But this one is in the mountains," Sarah responded, opening the magazine to the page she had marked. "It's this one," she added, pointing to a picture of a log cabin lodge and a group of women on the front porch proudly holding up their quilts.

Sarah slipped her reading glasses on and read the article aloud. "Quilting in the Great Smoky Mountains. Go back to a simpler time and enjoy the tranquility of the mountains as you learn about southern Appalachian culture while making a memory quilt. Relax on the porch, enjoying the spectacular mountain setting, or hike with local guides along the streams and through the forests to breathtaking scenic spots rarely seen by outsiders. Learn about mountain arts and crafts from local artisans while creating a quilt to display your fondest memories."

"So, Sophie. How about it? Do you want to go with me?" Sophie was Sarah's best friend, a short, rotund woman with an infectious laugh and the best friend a person could have.

"Me? I don't quilt. For that matter, I don't hike. I *do* sit on the porch and relax … but I can do that right here."

"So you don't want to go with me?"

"Well," Sophie began, sitting down at the table and picking up her third donut, "I'd probably go with you if it weren't for Higgy. He wants me to go to Alaska with him in the spring so he can meet Timmy, and I'd better save my traveling energy for that." The previous year, Sophie met Higgy, who described himself as a creative card consultant, although she later learned this was a major exaggeration. Higgy's real name was Cornelius Higginbottom, but Sophie announced that his name had entirely too many syllables for her taste, so she coined him Higgy.

"I can see that," Sarah responded. She knew Higgy was interested in becoming much more serious with her friend, and meeting Sophie's son was a good way to move that process forward. "If you change your mind, I'm sure I can get you in. Just let me know. You won't have to quilt; I promise."

Leaving Sophie's house, Sarah looked across the street and saw her previous home, now empty and with a *For Sale* sign in the small front lawn. She felt a moment of nostalgia, remembering all the times she and Sophie had scurried back and forth between their homes. Sarah and Charles now lived in their new house on the other side of the Village.

As she walked to the corner and headed up the street to her home in The Knolls, Sarah smiled to herself, remembering all the adjustments she and her new husband had made as they struggled with being newlyweds at their age. In their seventies, it was no easy task getting beyond their own habits and preferences. They were settled now and both wondered, in retrospect, why it had been so difficult.

Within minutes, Sarah was turning into Sycamore Court and heading toward her new home at the head of the cul-de-sac. When they got married the previous year, they had lived in Sarah's small attached house across from Sophie, but after a few months of needing more personal space, they decided to purchase a new house in their retirement community.

As she approached the front door, she smiled to realize how warm and inviting their home looked. The Village landscaper had offered a tree in front of each house and azaleas along the foundation. Charles left the choice up to her, and she chose a maple tree and coral azaleas. There was a small front porch with a railing where she added a long flower box, filled now with chrysanthemums since her summer flowers had faded and the days had become cooler.

"I'm home," she called out as she stepped into the living room. She was both surprised and pleased to find the front door unlocked. Cunningham Village had a security fence and security guards who patrolled the streets and manned the entry kiosk. She always felt safe there, but her husband, Charles, was a retired police officer and couldn't seem to set his suspicions aside. When they first met, he had insisted that she lock her door even when she walked her dog, Barney, on her own block. She hoped this unlocked door meant he was beginning to relax and let go of some of his law-enforcement habits.

"I'm back here," he hollered from the backyard. "How is Sophie doing?" Over the previous winter, after years of encouragement from her physicians and her friends, Sophie finally agreed to have her much-needed knee replacement. Despite her predictions of a catastrophic outcome, she sailed through the surgery and within a day was walking with the assistance of a walker and Higgy.

Cornelius, now called Higgy by all of Sophie's friends, moved into Sophie's guest room in order to take care of her for several weeks following her surgery and only recently moved back to his own house on the other side of Middletown.

"Health wise, she's doing great, but I think she misses Higgy. She enjoyed having him around." Barney got up and walked over to Sarah, pushing his head against her in greeting. *He's beginning to show his age*, she thought but didn't say. She had no idea how old he was when she got him from the pound, but the vet suggested he was perhaps seven or eight at the time. Charles was sitting on the ground next to Barney's doghouse adjusting the siding strips he had added to match their own house.

Barney returned to Charles' side, watching but not looking pleased. He had made it very clear that he neither needed nor wanted a doghouse. From the day Sarah brought him home, he had slept in his own bed in Sarah's room. He had reluctantly made one concession when she married Charles; he agreed to have his bed moved into the guest room. But as far as being outside in a green box, well, that was totally out of the question.

"I thought he asked her to marry him. What happened with that?" Charles asked, still mulling over the issue of Sophie and Higgy.

"She still hasn't answered him."

"He's waited over six months for an answer." he responded skeptically.

"Sure. I don't know about the quality back then, but I might be able to improve them with my photo software after they're converted. Just choose what you want and I'll take it from there."

Turning to the last page of the instructions, Sarah was pleased to see four quilt blocks to choose from for the alternating block: a Friendship Star, an Ohio Star, a simple Nine-Patch, and a Churn Dash. The fabric requirements were listed for each design and she took a deep breath, knowing that would be the easy part. She was eager to begin choosing her fabrics, but she wanted to get the photograph part out of the way first.

Charles brought all the albums into the kitchen and they sat down together to go through them. Choosing which pictures to use turned out to be a daunting task. She made tentative decisions, and then changed her mind several times. Finally, she realized she needed to know more about the project, so she did a computer search on memory quilts.

She browsed through the images and found quilts commemorating weddings, graduations, vacations, reunions, childhood, confirmation, trips, and even children's artwork. She also saw an overwhelming number of possible layouts and was glad they had mailed her the layout she would be using. *That's one decision I won't have to make*, she told herself.

After going through all their pictures, Sarah realized she needed to choose one category for now. She decided to use their wedding pictures. She knew Charles would like that and the quilt would include all her friends and family since they all attended the wedding. There were pictures of her daughter, Martha; and her son, Jason, with his wife, Jennifer, and their baby, Alaina. There were pictures of Sophie; Ruth and her sister, Anna; Andy and his daughter Caitlyn; and two of Charles' close friends from the police department. She decided to include a picture of Charles' son, John, with his wife and son even though they hadn't been at the wedding, but Sarah knew Charles would like having their picture on the quilt.

She had trouble picking one of herself since she never liked her own pictures. She decided to include the one that Charles liked best. She chose a few pictures from their honeymoon in Paris as well. She counted the pictures and found that she could easily pull together eighteen which would include all the family and their friends with a few extra of baby Alaina. After all those were chosen, Sarah went back through the pictures and chose one of her and Charles to place in the center of the quilt.

As her departure date grew close, Sarah began to feel a combination of excitement and apprehension. It had been several years since she traveled without Charles, but she had chosen to do this alone, despite the fact that husbands were welcome at the retreat center. She wanted to immerse herself in the experience without her natural tendency to worry about whether she should be spending more time with him. But she knew she would miss him. Married less than two years, they had developed a deep and loving bond.

Knowing it was too early to pack, Sarah was pulling together some of the things she thought she might need in the mountains and was making a list of what she needed to buy. As she was reaching for her fleece jacket on the top shelf of her closet while holding a pencil between her teeth, she heard the phone rang. "Charles? Can you get it?" she called out, garbling her words.

"Got it," he called from the living room. Walking into the bedroom with the phone, he said, "It's Sophie and she sounds very excited. She won't tell me what's going on. Here," he added handing the phone to his wife and removing the pencil from her mouth.

"Sophie! What's going on?" She hit the speaker button so that Charles could hear.

"Higgy wants to meet my son right away. We'd been talking about going next year, but all of a sudden he's in a hurry. Anyway, I called Tim and he agreed that we should fly to Alaska right away since it's a good time for him to take a few days off."

"That's terrific, Sophie. So you're going to do it?"

"Higgy already made the reservations," she squealed. "We're going in two weeks!"

"Two weeks. That's about when I'm leaving for my retreat. Can you get ready to leave that fast?"

"If you help me I can. Will you?"

"Of course, I will. What sort of help do you need?"

"I need help figuring out what to take. It'll be mid-September and probably cold in Alaska already, don't you think?"

"What does Timmy say?"

"I forgot to ask. Will you go on your computer and see what it'll be like up there in two weeks."

"I'll do it," Charles spoke up. "How long do you expect to be there?"

"No more than a couple of weeks, I would think. I forgot to ask Higgy. I'm so excited I can't think."

"Is Tim still in Valdez?" Charles asked, wondering what part of Alaska to look into. Tim has been working on the Alaska pipeline for the last forty years and is about ready to retire.

"Yes, he's right on Prince William Sound. It even sounds cold."

"That would be my guess, but I'll get the details for you."

Sarah and Sophie continued to talk excitedly about the details and, in comparing dates, realized they were leaving from the Hamilton airport one day apart, with Sophie leaving first.

"Okay Sophie," Sarah responded. "How about this? I'm in the process right now of making a list of what I'm taking and what I need to buy. When I finish here and as soon as Charles gets some weather information for us, I'll come over and we'll go through your closet and decide what to take. If you need more clothes, we'll run up to the mall tomorrow and do some shopping. By the way, how's your knee? Is it ready for a trip?"

"Absolutely. I called the doctor just to be sure and he said there was no reason I couldn't do it. He just said to keep up with the exercises, and we both know Higgy will see to it that I do them. He can be quite a nag. ..."

"Now, Sophie. You'll have to admit, you needed a bit of nagging when it came to those exercises, but it was worth it, wasn't it?"

"Yes, I'll admit it. I feel like a new person, but I miss my rhinestone cane."

"You can take it with you just in case, and it just might get you some preferential treatment along the way!" Sarah added with a chuckle.

"I don't think I'll mind missing my cane. I like the new me!"

* * * * *

Later that day, as the two friends sorted through Sophie's closet choosing items to take, Sarah started a list of a few things Sophie needed to buy. Charles had assured them she would need warm clothes; the temperature, he said, would range from the low-50s during the day to near freezing in the evening. They had chosen several outfits they felt would work along with her winter coat, a few sweaters, and a warm scarf. Sarah's list of things Sophie needed to purchase included a couple pair of warm slacks, a raincoat, warm boots, and two flannel nightgowns.

"And what's wrong with my elephant pajamas?" Sophie asked looking indignant.

"They're torn and have a grape juice stain all the way down one leg."

"They're still warm," Sophie said defiantly.

"You need two gowns," Sarah repeated firmly. "Do you have warm socks?"

As Sophie pulled socks out of her dresser drawer along with an assortment of underwear and the elephant pajamas, Sarah shook her head in defeat. She crossed out one of the flannel gowns. "When's Tim planning to retire?" she asked rather than deal with the pajama issue.

"He told his boss he's retiring at the end of the year. I guess we could have waited for them to meet, but Higgy is adamant about getting Tim's approval." With the look of a shy young girl, she added, "He's so cute when it comes to things like that. Sort of old-fashioned, you know?"

"Does this mean you've decided to marry him?"

Sophie was quiet and looked at Sarah with an expression more serious than Sarah had ever seen from her friend. "We'll see. ..."

Sarah reached over and hugged her and, to her surprise, Sophie hugged her back. Hugs were definitely not Sophie's forte.

"So what else do we need?" Sarah asked, returning to the pile of clothes. "Shoes? You have plenty of shoes, don't you?"

"Sure, but they're all old lady shoes."

"You'll be walking and you need stability with your new knee. I think your shoes are fine."

"They're old lady shoes," Sophie repeated.

"Let's look at them." Sarah pulled out the shoe rack and chose a brown pair and a black pair, both lace-up shoes. "What's wrong with these?"

"Aren't you listening? They're old lady shoes!"

"Do you want to look for some new ones? I think you'll be sorry if you do. You'll be walking much more than you're used to and these shoes are comfortable."

Sophie picked up the black pair. "They look like something my grandmother would wear."

"Your grandmother wore shoes laced above her ankles!" Sarah retorted. "Besides, new shoes can hurt," she added. "I have an idea. Let me take both of these over to Charles. After all those years in the police department, he's learned to make his shoes look like new. Let's see what he can do with them."

Sophie agreed to give it a try and Sarah tucked them into a bag and hurried out the door. Without thinking, she caught herself halfway across the street heading for her old house before she remembered she had moved. Turning back, she headed for her car in Sophie's driveway. As she passed the window, she saw Sophie shaking her head and smiling. *I miss living across the street from my friend*, Sarah told herself as she slid into the car.

The next day, Sarah and Sophie spent most of the day shopping. With the exception of a few things, they had cleared both of their lists. "We'll drive over to the mall in Hamilton closer to the time we're leaving," Sarah assured her when Sophie expressed concern that she still didn't have a raincoat.

Sarah drove Sophie to her door just as Higgy was driving up. "Come help me with my packages," Sophie called to him and he hurried over. Being only a couple of inches taller than Sophie, he easily leaned in and kissed her on the cheek before reaching for Sarah's hand.

"Thank you for taking care of my girl. I just didn't know how to advise her on this clothes thing."

"That's fine, Higgy. We had fun, and I think she's practically ready."

"See my new shoes?" Sophie said pulling her black shoes out of the bag they had just picked up from Charles. They sparkled like new and he had replaced the inner soles and shoe strings. Sophie beamed as she reached over and hugged Sarah. "Thanks," she muttered.

"That was probably the first hug Sophie ever initiated," Sarah told Charles when she arrived home. "Higgy is good for her."

"Love is what's good for her," Charles corrected.

"Love is what's good for everyone!" his wife responded as she kissed his cheek and headed for the kitchen to start dinner.

Chapter 3

"When does Sophie leave?" Charles asked one morning as they were having a late breakfast on the patio.

"Their flight is in the evening the day before I leave. He bought tickets on the red-eye; Sophie says she can sleep on the plane. I don't think I could."

"How are they getting to the airport?"

"They're driving. I guess they'll leave their car in long-term parking. Why do you ask?"

"Well, I had a thought. You're flying out in the afternoon of the next day, right?

"Yeah," she said curious as to what he had in mind.

"Why don't we drive them to Hamilton the day of their flight? We'll see them off and then we'll spend the night at that swanky hotel downtown. We can have a fancy dinner, a nice brunch the next morning, and make an embarrassing farewell scene at the airport in the afternoon."

"That's not a bad idea. I'll call Sophie and see what they think."

A few minutes later, Sarah returned saying they both loved the idea. "Higgy's been worried about leaving the new

SUV unattended for all that time. I'll call Caitlyn and see if she'll take care of Barney and Boots while we're gone."

Caitlyn was the daughter of their friend Andy. After a tumultuous childhood with her mother and stepfather, and a year spent living on the street at the young age of fourteen, she now had a stable, loving home with her father up the street from Sophie.

* * * * *

The next week flew by. As Sarah was putting the final touches on her packing, Charles sat on the bed looking like a lost puppy. "I'll miss you," he whimpered.

"Stop! You're a big boy, and I know you'll find plenty to entertain yourself." She knew there were lots of projects he wanted to tackle. "You could hang those shelves in the garage...."

"I'll miss you while I'm hanging them...."

"And then you wanted to find a better table for your computer ..."

"I hate shopping without you...." The lost puppy look was increasing with each suggestion.

Sarah sat down next to him and looked serious. "Are you really having trouble with me being away?"

Charles laughed. "I couldn't send you away without pouring on a little guilt, could I?"

"Well, I'll admit to feeling just a bit guilty even before your performance. It's our first year in our new home and part of me thinks I should be here with you."

"Of course not, sweetie!" he protested. "You should be doing exactly what you're doing. You love your quilting, and I'll bet you come home with several new classes for the shop."

She smiled feeling reassured and continued with her packing. "I wonder if I'll need a coat."

"I'd take something warm," he responded. "It could get cool in the evenings up there in the mountains, even though Tennessee is pretty far south."

"I'll take a jacket and my sweats. I can always layer." Sarah continued to fold her clothes and check off items from her list.

"How about fabric?"

"I packed that in my carry-on; I'm not taking any chances with lost luggage. Do you have any plans while I'm gone?"

Forgetting to look despondent about her being away, he responded enthusiastically. "I've set up a card game with the guys, and I'm thinking about talking to Matt about working on his new case. It involves some door-to-door interviewing over on the east side, and I'm sure he could use extra people." Matt Stokely was Charles' lieutenant when he was with the local police department and would outsource pieces of his investigations to retirees from time to time.

"So all that pouting was just to get my sympathy, huh? You're not only going to be fine, you're actually going to be having a great time."

"I guess so," he said looking guilty. "But I really will miss you."

"And I'll miss you," she told her new husband, still marveling that they were able to fall in love and make a life together at their age. After the children's father died and she sold their home to move into a retirement community, marriage was the last thing she would ever have predicted for herself. But here she was, in love and feeling like a youngster, at least when her arthritis wasn't reminding her that she was, in fact, getting older by the minute.

Charles suddenly jumped up and announced that he had completely forgotten to pack himself a bag for the overnight trip they were taking. It took some rushing around, but they were ready by 1:00 and drove first to Andy's house, picked up Caitlyn, gave her the key, and dropped her off in front of their house. Since it was the weekend, she had asked if she could spend the night with Barney and Boots. Andy agreed to the plan but told Charles he would be checking in on her that night. They then picked up Sophie and Higgy and the two couples left for Hamilton, an hour north of Middletown and the nearest airport.

Sophie was so excited, she couldn't stop talking. Charles asked if they would like to go to dinner with them since their plane didn't leave until late, but Higgy said they had already planned to get checked in and have dinner at the airport restaurant.

Sarah was somewhat relieved. As much as she loved her friend, she wanted to spend her last night in town with Charles. They had spent a romantic weekend at the same hotel the previous year and she thought it would be a nice send-off.

After they dropped Sophie and Higgy off at the airport and were checking into the hotel, the manager said, "Oh, Mr. Parker, you have a message." He pulled the note out of their reserved box and handed it to Charles along with their room key.

Call home right away, the note read. It was signed *Andy*.

"Home? Whose home? Our home?" Sarah asked apprehensively. They hurried up to the room and called their house. Andy picked up the phone right away.

"What's happened?" Charles asked anxiously.

"Sorry to worry you folks. Did you leave your washing machine running?"

Charles had the phone on speaker and Sarah gasped. "Oh no! I forgot that I was running a load of towels. Is it …?"

"It's pretty bad," Andy responded. "When Caitlyn walked in she noticed the dining room rug was squishy. She tracked it down to the washer that was still running with water flowing out. She called me and I told her how to turn the water off, but the kitchen is flooded and it's spreading into the other rooms. Do you want me to get the flood damage people out here? There're a few in the phone book here. …"

"Wait," Charles responded. "The water's off, right?"

"Yep, the water's turned off."

"I'll head on back to deal with it," he said, looking at Sarah questioningly.

"Of course. You need to go deal with this," Sarah responded. "I can take a cab to the airport tomorrow. I'm so sorry. This is all my fault; I never leave appliances running. I just got so caught up in …"

"Honey, please. Don't blame yourself. This was an accident that could happen to anyone. It can all be fixed."

"But our beautiful rugs …"

"That's what insurance is for. …"

A questioning "Hello?" came from the cell phone. Charles had forgotten Andy was waiting on the line.

"Oh, sorry, Andy. I'm coming on back but, in the meantime, I have a water vacuum in the garage. If you don't mind, would you just slurp up what you can so it doesn't spread any farther? I'll be there in a couple of hours."

"Okay," Andy responding, opening the garage door. "I see the water vac over in the corner, but don't you want me to go ahead and call one of those restoration companies?"

"Those places have 24-hour service. I'll call when I get there. I'll contact the insurance company from here and give them a heads-up. They might even want me to call a specific outfit. By the way, how's Barney taking all this?"

"He's almost as upset as Caitlyn. Now, your cat's a different story. She's asleep on top of the kitchen cabinet."

They talked a few more minutes and as they were hanging up, Andy said, "Hold on a second, Charles." Obviously turning to speak to Caitlyn, Andy asked, "What is it honey?" After a brief period, Andy returned to the phone. "Caitlyn says Boots is just fine, but she doesn't think we should leave Barney here. He's really stressed. Is it okay if she walks him back to our house?"

From the background, Sarah spoke up saying, "Of course, that's fine. Thank you Caitlyn for taking care of him, and Boots will be fine right there. She would be more upset if you tried to take her out. Charles will be on his way soon." Turning to Charles, she again said, "I'm so sorry about all this. …"

He told Andy he was on his way and pulled Sarah to his side, gently kissing the top of her head. "No worries, sweetie. I don't want this to ruin your trip."

"The trip!" she exclaimed. "I shouldn't go. I should go back with you and …"

"No! Absolutely not! These are all things I can handle, and if I have any questions, I'll call you. If we need to buy new rugs, I'll file the claims and we'll go out and do that when you get home. And the washer is under warranty. If we need new tiles, I'll go ahead and have the same ones installed. Okay?"

"I feel terrible about leaving you with all this," she said apologetically.

Charles hugged her and with a chuckle said, "And you were afraid I wouldn't have enough to keep me busy!"

Chapter 4

"Are you on your way to Ten Oaks Lodge?"

Sarah, sipping coffee in the Knoxville airport lounge, looked up to see a trim woman with salt-and-pepper hair approaching her table. She was carrying a quilted tote bag and wearing a jacket that had been pieced with squares of pale pastel. *This woman is a quilter*, Sarah thought as she smiled and responded. "Yes, I am. Are you my ride?"

Sarah's plane had arrived in Knoxville earlier than expected, and she was waiting for a representative from the retreat center. They were offering shuttle services for their participants to and from the airport. "No, I'm waiting as well. Actually, I just guessed that you might be a quilter. I noticed your Caribbean-style tote bag and it looked similar to one I made on a quilting cruise several years ago."

"That's where I made mine," Sarah exclaimed. The woman introduced herself as Holly Harper and Sarah invited her to sit down. The two women compared notes about their quilting cruises and both agreed it was something they would love to do again.

"Have you been to any of this company's retreats?" Sarah asked. "I really have no idea what to expect."

"You'll be very pleased with it, I'm sure," Holly responded. "Last year I went to one in Lancaster County. We were a small group and we stayed in a lodge, but they had rented a house and barn from an Amish family for the quilting during the day. We were without electricity and other conveniences. We used treadle machines to make small quilts and then we grouped around quilting frames in the barn and hand quilted our projects."

"Was it hard to get used to the treadle machine?"

"At first it was. I had trouble getting a steady rhythm going, but once I caught on, I got pretty good at it. It made me think about my grandmother and all the sewing she did on hers. I still have it up in the attic. I keep thinking I'll get it down and use it, but you know how that is. Anyway, we had a good time at the retreat."

"What did you make?"

"I was working on a baby quilt for my granddaughter. The friend I went with made an exquisite wall hanging. She and I worked together to do the quilting. I really got a feel for the camaraderie the Amish women must feel when they're quilting together. While we worked, local women came in and talked to us about their quilting and their traditions. The whole experience was fascinating and I learned so much!"

"You were experiencing quilting the way it was for our grandmothers."

"True, but when I got home I really appreciated my computerized sewing machine and Judy, my long-arm quilter," Holly confessed looking a bit guilty.

"From the brochures and comments from previous participants," Sarah said, "it looks like this retreat will be similar. It mentions that local musicians and artisans will be coming in. I'm very excited."

About that time, a fit-looking man appearing to be in his mid-sixties walked up to the table. Holly turned to greet him and said, "Sarah, this is my husband, Drew. Drew, this is Sarah Parker. She's on her way to the retreat as well."

"How do you do, Mrs. Parker. Is your husband with you?" he added looking around the immediate area.

"No. He stayed home to take care of the pets and, as it turned out, to remove standing water from the main floor of our new home." Drew Harper sat down and signaled to the waitress for a cup of coffee. Sarah explained about the washing machine catastrophe, and the three commiserated.

"Are you going to be quilting with us?" Sarah asked Drew.

Drew laughed and responded, "Oh no. That's all Holly's department. My job is to carry the machine and boxes of supplies and fabric. I got off easy this time—no machines to carry!" Machines were being provided so that travelers wouldn't have to bring their own.

"So you'll just be relaxing and enjoying the mountain air?"

"Actually, I've located a hiking group up here. Back home I hike with a local hiking club and we're encouraged to get together with other clubs whenever we're traveling." Looking at his wife, he added with a chuckle, "Well, I said *we*, but if there's a quilting activity within fifty miles of the hike, it's just me."

"Hiking up here in the mountains should be beautiful," Sarah commented.

"And treacherous!" Holly added, patting her husband's arm. "You watch that ankle of yours."

Giving his wife an appreciative look, Drew said, "We'll be following the Appalachian Trail from Gatlinburg south. There's a shuttle that'll bring us back at the end of the hike." Looking toward the entrance, he added, "Speaking of shuttles, I'll bet this is our ride."

Drew stood to meet the young man who was heading their way. Neatly dressed in jeans and a Ten Oaks Lodge tee-shirt, he asked, "Are you the folks going to Ten Oaks?"

"We sure are," Drew answered extending his hand. "I'm Drew Harper; this is my wife, Holly, and our new friend, Mrs. Palmer."

Sarah smiled and shook the young man's hand. "It's Parker," she corrected. "Sarah Parker, and your name?"

"Hi. I'm Coby Slocum. The van's out front. Did you folks already pick up your bags?"

"Yes, they're right here," Drew answered, pointing toward the baggage cart where he had stacked all their suitcases.

As they walked through the terminal, Sarah asked Coby how far they were from the lodge.

"Ten Oaks is just outside Gatlinburg. It took me about an hour to get here."

Just making conversation, she asked how long Coby had been with the lodge. "I've been working there for two years, since I graduated high school. My sister, Mary Beth, works in the kitchen; and Dad is the general manager."

"This is a real family affair, isn't it?"

"It sure is," Coby responded, beginning to load the bags into the back of the van. "My grandpa is chopping wood for the fireplaces right now."

In preparation for the retreat, Sarah had been reading about life in the southern Appalachian Mountains, and one thing she learned was that you can't make assumptions about people living in the mountains. Some actually fit the stereotype and are living in dilapidated shacks, are illiterate, and extremely poor; but others are educated and making a good living, particularly in and around the small mountain villages. But whether privileged or poor, they were all described as very proud people. Sarah was born in the Midwest and knew that was something she shared with mountain folks here. They were known to be proud, independent people who didn't accept charity and who took care of their own.

For the first part of their trip, they were driving through a valley surrounded by a hilly terrain on all sides, but as they headed toward Gatlinburg, they began to climb. As the valley fell below them, they continued up the winding roads. "What's the elevation at the lodge?" she asked Coby.

"I don't know about the elevation, but it's way up there for sure. It's just on the edge of the Great Smoky Mountains National Park, and those mountains are said to be five or six thousand feet. You can ask in the park; you'll probably spend some time there. Most folks do."

"That's where we start our hike," Drew announced. "We're going up to some dome which is supposed to be an excellent overlook. ..."

"That's Clingman's Dome!" Coby responded enthusiastically. "You gotta see that!"

The group settled into their seats and enjoyed Coby's very competent driving through the foothills and small towns. Sarah spotted several barns with large wooden quilt blocks displayed on the sides, but Coby didn't know anything about them. "Ask at the lodge," he suggested. "They know all this stuff."

Thirty or so minutes of driving brought them into the resort town of Pigeon Forge. "Anyone need a break?" Coby asked, but the group chose to keep going. A few more miles of driving brought them into, and quickly beyond, the small resort town of Gatlinburg that was surrounded on all sides by high mountain ridges. "You folks will be coming back here to look around," Coby announced. "We're pretty close now." Sarah could feel the altitude and was silenced by the incredible beauty.

The road became narrow with hairpin turns as the group progressed toward their destination. The van hugged the mountain on their right as the group nervously looked at the drop on the left. Sarah realized there was no railing and nothing to prevent them from tumbling to their death. Oblivious to the dangers Sarah was imagining, Coby spoke up saying, "You folks mind if I stop and pick up my baby sister?"

Sarah, sitting in the front seat with Coby, swallowed hard and looked away from the precipice. Glancing back at the Harpers, she saw they were pale but were nodding their agreement. "Sure," Sarah responded. "Where is she?"

"She's right up the road a bit. I take her to the lodge when I can. She likes to hang around with my sister there and it'll give Mama a break, what with the new baby."

Coby took the next right and followed a rutted dirt road back into the woods. He took a left and began climbing farther up the mountain. The trees were thick, reaching out across the road and forming a heavy canopy that blocked out the sky. One more turn and they were in a clearing in front of a modern log cabin nestled in the trees and facing out over the valley. Sarah gasped at the breathtaking view.

"Hey, Coby!" hollered a little girl about five as she ran toward the car. She wore a cotton dress and sneakers and looked freshly scrubbed. "Mama said I can go," she announced excitedly, but then realized there were strangers in the car, and she flattened herself against the car on the driver's side, hanging her head with embarrassment.

"Move away so I can open the door, Sissy." Coby stepped out, picked her up, and headed for the back of the van.

"She can sit by me," Sarah called. "There's plenty of room."

"Are you sure?" Coby asked, knowing he wasn't supposed to inconvenience the guests in any way.

"Absolutely. Come on, sweetie, sit by me."

"Thank you," the little girl responded in a near whisper as she took her place between Sarah and her brother. She was quiet and sat very still all the way to the lodge despite Sarah's attempts at conversation.

"She's very shy," her brother explained.

Another ten-minute drive brought them to a marker for Ten Oaks. Turning right onto the country lane, they traveled another few miles, again weaving up the mountain side.

Near the top, they came to a large wooden sign announcing the entrance to Ten Oaks Lodge and Retreat Center. As Coby turned on the entry road, Sarah was astounded by the beauty of the secluded setting. The log cabin lodge sat directly ahead of her looking larger and more magnificent than it had appeared in the brochures. "This is it?" she asked breathlessly.

"This is it," Coby responded proudly as he pulled to a stop in the parking lot. Loading their bags onto the waiting cart, he led them into the lodge and toward the desk in the lobby. "Start over here," he advised as he lined their bags up by the desk.

Later, watching Holly and Drew heading for their room arm in arm, Sarah had a pang of regret that Charles wasn't with her. Feeling lonely, she headed to her room, almost sorry she hadn't opted for a roommate, but once she opened the door and saw the pile of quilts on the beds, she knew she would relish her solitude in this cozy mountain space.

* * * * *

It was early evening and there were no retreat plans until 9:00 the next morning. After a light supper in the dining room, Sarah approached the desk clerk, holding out her cell phone and said, "I can't seem to get a signal. Do cell phones work up here?"

"Most of the time, yes. But it's sporadic. Try out on the porch. If that doesn't work, just try again after a while. The weather affects it up here sometimes." It was a beautiful autumn day with a mild nip in the air. Sarah couldn't imagine how the weather could be interfering with the signal today. She walked out to the porch and was astounded by the view. Beyond their wooded ridge, Sarah could see the rolling mountains tinged with shades of hazy blue that melded into the sky in the far distance. She was momentarily speechless, but finally took a deep breath and dialed again.

"Hi, babe. You got there!" Charles answered, sounding relieved to get her call.

"I sure did and now I'm sorry I discouraged you from coming. You would love it!"

"It's just as well. There were things to take care of here."

Feeling a pang of guilt, Sarah asked, "How is the house?"

"Not as bad as I thought. The guys brought in huge fans and the carpet should be dry in another twenty-four hours. They did most of the work actually. They mopped up the tile floors in the kitchen and cleaned them with a disinfectant. Except for these monster fans and more noise than a jet taking off, we're pretty much back to normal."

As Sarah was talking, she saw Sissy walking around in the parking lot. Probably waiting for her brother, she thought.

"How's Barney taking it?" she said to Charles, thinking about all the noise.

"Andy and Caitlyn kept him over there. He slept last night with Caitlyn so now he knows about sleeping on the bed instead of by it. I guess we'll have some explaining to do when he gets home."

Sarah laughed and asked about Boots.

"Still on top of the kitchen cabinet. I climbed up on a chair and fed her. She has her water dish and some toys. I tossed her blanket up there with her. She may just live up there; she seems perfectly happy with the arrangement."

"How about her litter?"

"It's on top of the refrigerator. She'll venture that far away from her new home."

"I sure hope that's back on the floor by the time I get home," she said frowning.

They continued to talk for the next twenty minutes. She told him about the flight and the drive to Ten Oaks. She promised to take pictures of the lodge and the view from the porch the next day and send them to his cell phone. They said good night just as dusk was settling in and she could see the moon over the mountains. "This place takes your breath away," she said as they were hanging up.

As she turned to go into the lodge, she caught sight of something moving in the thicket just beyond the driveway. "Is someone there?" she called out but there was no answer. It was getting dark and it was difficult to see into the woods, but she was sure she saw movement. *Surely Coby's little sister knows better than to wander off into the woods*, she assured herself.

Sarah went down the steps and walked over to the edge of the woods. Again she called out, "Hello? Is someone there?" She heard the rustling again, but this time it seemed to be farther away. She looked back at the lodge and considered going for help, but she didn't want to appear foolish. Whoever or whatever it was had moved farther into the woods. *Probably just an animal*, she told herself, but still wondered if it could have been Sissy. She went into the lodge still not sure if she should tell someone.

She was pleased to spot Sissy and her sister coming out of the kitchen and heading for the side door where Coby was waiting. *So it wasn't Sissy*, she thought thankfully.

She tried to forget the incident, but sleep was slow to come.

Chapter 5

Sarah woke up at 5:00 and couldn't go back to sleep. Breakfast wasn't going to be served until 7:30. She got up, took a shower, and dressed. *Now what*, she wondered. She considered taking a walk but was still feeling a bit spooked from the night before. Remembering her bag of fabrics, she decided to take them out and look at them again. She loved handling fabric and was eager to meet the other women and see what fabrics they had chosen.

It was still early, so she pulled out all the written materials she had received from Ten Oaks and reread all the instructions, feeling comfortable that she was completely prepared. The retreat center was providing machines for its out-of-town participants as well as most of the supplies they would need for cutting, measuring, and pressing. She only had to bring her photo disk, fabric, and coordinating thread for her project. There were going to be several other small projects, but the center was providing all the materials.

At 7:15, she realized it was time to go downstairs to the dining room. She left her fabrics spread out on the extra bed and grabbed her jacket in case she needed it. In the hallway, she met Holly and they walked down the wide staircase together. "Is Drew joining us for breakfast?"

"He was up and out at 6:00 this morning. The group was meeting at a campground for a breakfast cookout!"

"That sounds like fun," Sarah remarked, imagining the smell of a wood fire and bacon cooking.

"Sounds cold to me," Holly responded, pulling her sweater tight around her. "It's freezing this morning!"

Sarah was comfortable and wondered if Holly was accustomed to a warmer climate. "We're from southern Florida," Holly responded when Sarah asked, "and I'm not used to this frigid weather." Once they entered the dining room, Holly headed straight for the coffee bar. She filled a large mug with steaming coffee, which she then used as a hand warmer. "There. That's better," she said joining Sarah at one of the tables set for four. They were joined by another woman who introduced herself as Jane, and the three women chatted excitedly about the retreat.

An elderly woman entered the room looking around as if lost. "Jane?" she called out.

"Mom, over here," Jane called to her. Turning to Sarah and Holly as she stood up, Jane said, "I was watching for her, but I got so caught up in … Mom, over here …" Looking relieved, she added, "Here she comes now. Mother, this is Sarah and Holly, and this is my mother, Genevieve. Let's stick with first names if that's okay with you folks. It's easier for Mom."

Jane's mother sat down next to Jane but looked anxious. "Why are we sitting down?" she asked her daughter.

"We're going to have breakfast, Mom. Do you want coffee?"

"I don't see any coffee," she responded looking around anxiously.

"I'll get it for you. Just wait here." As Jane stood up and walked to the courtesy coffee bar, her mother got up and followed her. "Mom, go back and sit down." Her mother looked around not knowing what to do.

Sarah decided to help her back to the table, but Genevieve was reluctant to go with her. "Who are you?" Genevieve asked nervously. "I don't know you."

"This may have been a mistake," Jane said returning to the table with a cup of coffee and her mother in tow. "My sister couldn't take her and I couldn't bring myself to cancel the retreat. Here Mom, here's your coffee just the way you like it."

"Thank you, and stop treating me like a child," her mother responded looking annoyed.

A dozen more women had entered the room and found seats at three other tables. A young man took drink orders while the waitress served breakfast family style. Each table received a platter piled high with bacon, sausage links, and ham slices, a bowl of fluffy scrambled eggs, and a basket of biscuits. The room became electrified as the four tables of women ate and talked excitedly about their upcoming experience.

Halfway through breakfast, Jane's mother said she wanted to go to her room. "Excuse me," Jane said standing. "I'll be right back." She helped her mother up and guided her toward the first floor rooms beyond the dining room and lobby.

"That's hard," Holly said shaking her head. "I was talking to Jane last night. Her mother's been diagnosed with dementia, most likely Alzheimer's. They have a rough road ahead of them."

"Does her mother live with her?"

"Jane moved into her mother's house to care for her. They were both alone and she said it seemed less disruptive to her mom if she stayed in her familiar home. Jane sold her house."

"There's a sister she mentioned. ..."

"Not much help, from what I gathered."

"It's rough," Sarah responded as she picked at the remainder of her meal. About that time Jane returned.

"Okay, she's settled for a while. It's amazing how that woman can just close her eyes and fall right to sleep. She'll nap for a couple of hours."

"Will she be okay alone?"

"I think so. I talked to Chuck at the desk. He said the front door is monitored at all times. He'll let me know if she comes into the lobby."

"What about while you're sewing?" Holly asked, realizing that Genevieve could be quite a distraction to Jane.

"She enjoys projects and she quilted all her life. I think we'll be able to work on our quilt together. We went through the pictures and she was very interested in the idea of a memory quilt. I'm making this one for her."

"What a wonderful idea!" Sarah responded. "You can regularly look at the pictures with her and talk about old times. ..."

"Exactly!"

Sarah privately tossed the idea around in her head. She wondered if that might be a service the quilt shop could offer quilters as a way of helping them with their caregiving responsibilities. She could immediately think of several customers who often talked about the dilemma of caring for parents with serious memory problems.

After breakfast, the group was directed to the conference room that would be their classroom for the next ten days.

"Will your mother be able to find us?" Sarah asked as the women walked toward the classroom.

"I requested a room on the first floor close to the classroom. I'll be able to go out the side door and right to our room to keep an eye on her. She sleeps quite a bit during the day; unfortunately, she's up most of the night, so you girls might have to help keep me awake in class!" she added with a good-natured chuckle.

The conference room that was being used as their classroom was spacious, and each participant had a six-foot worktable. Two attractively dressed women, probably in their late fifties, were circulating around the room greeting the participants as they came in. After everyone was seated, the women introduced themselves as Brenda and Cheryl. They passed out name tags and markers and suggested that everyone put just their first names on the tags. "It's much easier that way," Cheryl said with a knowing smile and she received unanimous agreement from the group.

Brenda talked for a few minutes about the lodge and its amenities. She explained about meals and said that today's breakfast was the only meal that would be served family style. She passed out menus and meal cards. "You check off what you want the next day for breakfast and lunch. Dinners will be buffet style. The times are printed on the menu."

"What about lunch today?" one of the women asked.

"Oh, sorry. Lunch today will be served on the road." Looking surprised, everyone looked around to see if they had missed something. "You look surprised!" Brenda said with a mischievous smile. "Well, this was a last-minute change in our schedule. We learned just yesterday that Mary Ellen McPherson will be doing a trunk show in Knoxville and we were able to arrange for a bus to take us. Now, I know many of you have been on the road, so you're welcome to stay here and relax if you prefer, but it's open to everyone and, of course, we've covered all the costs."

"Do you know Mary Ellen McPherson?" Sarah asked Holly.

"I read an article about her in a quilting magazine. She does art quilts and they're amazing. Not really my style, but she wins awards all over the country for her fabric art."

"Are you going?" Sarah asked.

"I guess. It'll be a rare experience since we don't get celebrities in my small town. I'm tired though, and I'm tempted to stay here and just take a walk around the grounds."

"I hate to pass up an opportunity like this," Sarah responded thoughtfully, "but a relaxed afternoon in this serene setting really appeals to me too. I think I'll stay behind. I wonder if we can get lunch here."

Anticipating the question, Brenda said, "For those who stay behind, there'll be a salad bar in the dining room." She then added, "I've put a sign-up sheet on the front desk. Anyone who wants to go, please add your name. The bus will be here at 11:30 and you'll be back here before dinnertime. Let's take a quick break so anyone interested can sign up."

Once everyone was again seated, Cheryl said, "Let's get down to the really important stuff. Our retreat!" Everyone clapped encouraging her to continue. "We'll be meeting here every day after breakfast and we'll work all day unless we have an outside activity. After dinner, the room will be open until midnight. You're welcome to come down and sew in your pajamas if you want."

"Also," Brenda spoke up from the sideline, "Cheryl and I are here for you. Don't hesitate to come to either of us with questions, problems, … anything you need.

"What about outside activities?" a participant to Sarah's left called out.

"Ah. We need to talk about that," Cheryl responded. "Well, first of all there's the trunk show this afternoon. Then the day after tomorrow we'll spend the whole day out. We're going to the Smoky Mountain Crafts Museum where you'll see samples of many of the arts and crafts common to the area. They also have vendor spaces where artisans sell their own crafts. We've arranged to go on a day when most of the artists will be there so you can meet them and ask questions."

"Do they have quilts there?" Jane asked.

"Lots of quilts! And a few special displays this month. We'll have lunch in their cafeteria and leave there in the midafternoon. We'll be driving from there through the Great Smoky Mountain National Park and stopping to view the area from Clingman's Dome. From there …"

"Excuse me," one of the younger quilters in the group said. "What's Clingman's Dome?"

"Sorry. I got ahead of myself. It's an observation tower in the park. I've heard you can see for a hundred miles from the dome. When I was there, there was too much haze to see that far, but it was still spectacular. There are brochures on the table at the back of the room about the museum and Clingman's Dome. Help yourself."

"Okay, from there, we'll stop for dinner in a local restaurant where you'll get the best food you ever ate!"

"So, let me see. Brenda, what else is on our schedule?"

"Well, let's see. There's a trip into Gatlinburg for shopping. ..."

"Fabric shopping?" someone asked and everyone laughed.

"Of course, fabric shopping," she responded with a knowing grin. "And any other kind of shopping you're interested in." Turning to Brenda again, she asked, "What else do we have on the agenda?"

"Just the play," Brenda responded.

"Yes," Cheryl responded enthusiastically. "That's on the sixth day of the retreat. A local high school is performing *The American Quilt* and it should be delightful. These kids have a talented drama department."

After a few questions and some chatting between tables, Brenda announced, "Let's get down to the nitty-gritty about our project." She then talked about the photographs and requested that everyone bring their disks the next morning. "I'll be giving them to the staff for printing while we begin making our quilt blocks. They'll have them back to us the next morning."

"What size will they be?" one of the students asked.

"They'll be standard five-by-seven inches and we'll add fabric strips to the sides to make them eight-and-a-half inches square. The photos and the pieced blocks will all be eight inches finished."

"Will we be setting them the way they were in the pictures you sent us?" one of the students asked.

"Yes." Brenda pulled three quilts out of her bag and Cheryl helped her clip them onto the display frames. "Come up and look closely if you'd like."

The blocks were placed five across and seven down with eighteen pictures alternating with seventeen pieced blocks. Sarah studied the pieced blocks and was confused by the way they were done. Only one was done the way she intended to do hers with the same quilt block repeated for all of the pieced blocks. The second one was completed like a sampler, using the four that were included with the instructions plus thirteen other block designs that weren't on the list. The third had the Churn Dash block, but instead of following the pattern, the Churn Dash was made smaller and placed on point with setting blocks in the corners to make it square. Sarah wondered if she had misunderstood the instructions, but then realized one of the three samples repeated the same block like she planned to do.

"I notice you have varied from the instruction sheet," she started saying, when another woman spoke up as well saying, "… and these samples scare me! I don't think I can do all that work in ten days."

Cheryl was smiling and shaking her head. "I'm really sorry about this. The instructions we sent you are correct. You can change it if you want, but we'll be instructing by the layout we sent you. All you'll need to do is choose a quilt block and make seventeen of them. The confusion came when we asked a local quilt club to make three sample quilts for us and these are what we received," she added looking toward Brenda to finish.

"They're a very competitive group," Brenda added laughing. "Very competitive, and they were trying to outdo each other. But this is the layout we'll be using," she said, pointing to the first one. It had photo blocks alternating with only one of the blocks from the instruction sheet.

Cheryl continued saying, "Now, we know that we have a few very experienced quilters at this retreat, and you're welcome to modify the pattern any way you want."

"Is everyone clear on what we're doing?" Brenda asked and the group nodded.

"Let's stop here and get to know each other." One by one, the students introduced themselves, talked a little about their experience, and displayed their fabric choices. *Cheryl was right*, Sarah thought. *We have some very experienced quilters here!*

* * * * *

A golden harvest moon was perched just behind the mountain range as Sarah sat on the porch to call Charles. It was hard to believe this same moon was shining on her house back home. She wanted to tell Charles about it, but found it indescribable. She used her cell phone to snap a picture, but was disappointed that it didn't reveal the true beauty of the moment. She decided not to send it and just keep the memory in her heart.

"Hi, sweetie," he answered. They talked awhile about their day. She told him about deciding to skip the field trip and just relax around the lodge. She'd wanted to follow a nature trail through the woods but realized she was still feeling a bit squeamish. She hadn't told Charles about the previous night and decided not to mention it. Instead, she told him about her afternoon.

"I treated myself to a soak in the Jacuzzi. It's out on the back porch and it was only about sixty degrees today. I thought I'd freeze, but when I stepped in the water it was very warm, steaming in fact, and it felt wonderful. I stayed out there in the sun and soaked until I was a prune!"

"… and you were wearing …?" he asked playfully.

"Charles! Shame on you," she responded. "I brought my bathing suit."

"What else did you do with your afternoon off?"

"I took a nap and, after that soak, it was a great nap."

"I'm glad you had some relaxing time, sweetie." Charles then told her he had purchased shelving and brackets for the garage, wanting to organize his tools and guy stuff, as Sarah called them. "I also got boards to put a rudimentary floor in the attic so I can put some of our storage up there."

"Like what?" Sarah asked, wondering what they had that could be put away that inconveniently.

"Those boxes of mine in the garage mainly. I'm afraid to leave them out there another winter. They just might get damp and mildewed."

"The boxes in the corner? What's in those boxes?"

Charles hesitated a moment, but then said, "Just some case stuff I kept when I retired."

"From the department?" she asked surprised that he had kept anything. "What are you going to do with them?"

"For now, I'm putting them in the attic."

"No, I mean why did you keep them?"

Again, he hesitated. "There're a few cases that I worked on that were never solved. They just stuck in my craw. I wanted to hang onto my notes and copies of some of the paperwork. You never know. ..."

"Never know what?" Sarah asked, still wondering what this was all about.

"Okay. Sometimes one of the new guys will pick up a cold case and see if fresh eyes can see something the original guys missed. If that ever happens on these cases, I want to be involved. These cases meant more to me than most, you know?"

Sarah could hear the concern in his voice. "You'll have to tell me about them when I get home."

"I will. Now on to better stuff. Did you find out how they'll be transferring your pictures to fabric?"

"Not yet. We won't be talking about that until tomorrow, so I'll know more then. How are the kids doing?"

Charles knew she was talking about their animals, Barney and Boots. "Well, Barney's back home. Once the fans were removed and the house was back to normal, I went over and got him."

"Was he happy to see you?"

"You bet, but he looked behind me and seemed disappointed that you weren't there. Then when we got back to the house, he lumbered from room to room. I'm sure he was looking for you. I tried to explain, but he settled down as soon as Boots came down from the cabinet. I guess he felt he had to be brave for her benefit."

They laughed about the pets when suddenly Charles said, "Oh, did Sophie call you?"

"No, not that I know of. Was she going to?"

"She called here this morning. She forgot to take your cell phone number. I figured she was going to call you."

"Maybe I'll give her a call tomorrow. Right now I only have a couple of bars so the signal is very weak."

They continued to chat for a few minutes, neither really wanting to break the connection, but ultimately there was some interference on the line, and Sarah said she should hang up. Returning to her room, she sat down and thought about Charles and his cases, knowing he would never really be retired. He was a cop through and through.

As she was getting into bed, the phone rang. Since it wasn't her cell phone, she assuming it was probably someone inside the hotel.

"Sarah, hi. It's Ruth. How's it going?"

"Ruth?" Sarah had to pause a second to get oriented, not expecting to hear from the owner of the quilt shop back home. "Are you okay?" she asked.

"I'm fine and I shouldn't be bothering you, but I can't possibly wait until you get home to find out about the project. I'm excited about the idea of offering a memory-quilt class at the shop and wanted to see if you still like the idea."

Sarah laughed. "Well, first things first," she said. "We haven't started sewing yet but I'm beginning to think we can do this!" She went on to describe the sample quilts and the process.

"How do you get the pictures onto the fabric? I've heard that's a long, drawn-out process."

"Not anymore," Sarah responded. "You can buy fabric in sheets all prepared and ready to go through an inkjet printer."

"Wonderful! We can even do that for them," Ruth exclaimed.

"Or, Anna's husband can do it," Sarah added. "You mustn't forget you have a computer whiz in the family." Anna was Ruth's sister. She helped in the shop and processed the online orders that Ruth received through the website Anna's husband set up for her.

"You're right," Ruth squealed with excitement. "I can't wait to get started. This would be an excellent class to offer our customers. We're all sick of sticking pictures into albums or losing them to the bottom of a box."

"I agree. It'll be a fun thing to do, but it could also be a very useful tool."

"How so?" Ruth asked sounding curious.

"Well, one of the women brought her mother with her to the retreat. The mother is experiencing signs of dementia. Jane brought family pictures and is making the memory quilt for her mother as a way of helping her keep her memories fresh."

"Interesting idea," Ruth said, turning the concept over in her mind. After a short pause, she added, "It would be an excellent class for many reasons. I'm eager to talk about this when you get home."

As they were saying good night, Ruth said, "Oh, I just remembered the time difference. I've kept you up. I'm sorry."

"No problem, Ruth. I'm glad you called."

Sarah pulled the covers up and glanced at the clock, remembering that breakfast was served promptly at 7:30. Yawning, she turned out the light. She had left the window shades up so she could see the moon shining through the trees. Somewhere off in the distance, she heard an animal howl and another respond.

Sarah smiled as she drifted off to sleep.

Chapter 6

Sitting at her worktable the next morning, Sarah spread out her fabrics, eager to begin working on her quilt. She had chosen the Ohio Star block, thinking that it would complement her wedding pictures. Before coming to the retreat, Sarah had spent several hours at the fabric store choosing her fabrics and had settled on a delicate fabric that featured soft white blossoms with touches of navy gracefully floating on a background of aqua and lavender. She decided to use this as her focus fabric for her outer border. For her Ohio Star block, she found a tone-on-tone lavender for the stars and a pale aqua for the star background. She chose a navy for the quilt's inner border and decided to buy enough navy to outline her photographs as well.

"What are you thinking about so hard over there?" Jane asked, noticing that Sarah was studying her fabrics with a frown.

"I'm hoping my fabrics are right," she responded beginning to look worried. "Maybe I should have a different background for my blocks." She spread out her fabrics and told them her plan. "And I'm also wondering about this navy ..."

"They're beautiful," Jane exclaimed.

"They are," Holly chimed in. "Are these the colors of your wedding?"

"Actually, it was a very simple wedding, but my daughter wore aqua and my matron of honor wore lavender and I think these fabrics will complement the photographs nicely."

"I think they'll be perfect," Jane's mother spoke up surprising everyone. "And the Ohio Star is one of my favorite blocks. Did you know it was also called the Tippecanoe and Tyler Too block?"

Sarah looked surprised and said, "No. Why do you suppose?"

"Well," Genevieve continued, "It was back during the 1840 presidential campaign. It was the slogan for William Harrison and John Tyler, and this quilt block was their symbol."

"Fascinating," Sarah responded glancing at Jane to see how she was responding to her mother's sudden lucidity, but Jane was sorting her own fabrics at the time and didn't seem at all surprised. Turning back to Genevieve, Sarah asked, "Do you know why they used that slogan?"

"It just so happens I do know," she responded with a satisfied grin. "William Harrison was known for his victory against the Indians at the battle of Tippecanoe. That was in the early 1800s," she added looking at Jane for clarification. "About 1814, don't you think?" she asked her daughter.

"I have no idea, Mother. You're the family expert on historical trivia."

"Trivia? This is important stuff, my dear." The two bantered awhile before settling down to work on their blocks.

I haven't, Sarah thought. "Let me know what you find out. I'm not going to tell Sophie you're looking into it just yet."

"Does this Higginbottom person have any kind of plan for straightening this out?" Charles asked.

"No. Sophie said he's still sitting around mumbling that he didn't think it would count."

"I hope your friend rethinks her plans. This guy worries me." With a sarcastic chuckle he added, "I wonder if he was marrying Sophie in Alaska because he thought that wouldn't count either."

"Now, Charles. He may be a doofus like you said last week, but I don't think he'd intentionally hurt Sophie. I think he seriously cares for her."

As Sarah headed back toward the lodge, she felt like she was being watched, but she was too concerned about Sophie to take it seriously, telling herself it was just her imagination.

She continued walking at a quickened pace and was relieved when she could hear the sounds of the lodge just ahead. As she stepped out of the woods, she saw a group of people climbing out of a minibus with lettering on the side that said *Sounds of the Mountains*.

Sarah wasn't much in the mood for sewing, but fortunately, as she reached the room, her class was in the process of breaking for the day. "Don't forget to join us on the front porch after dinner for a good ol' mountain jamboree," Brenda was saying.

* * * * *

Sarah heard the music from her room and hurried downstairs. She met Jane and Holly in the lobby and the three went out on the front porch. The sun was setting behind the mountains and canvas chairs had been set up on the porch along with a refreshments table. The band was playing in the parking lot just below.

The band consisted of three men and a woman. Looking like something out of the 70s, the men had long hair and unruly beards. All three wore tank tops despite the cool evening, but by the end of the night, they were dripping with sweat. Playing banjos and guitars, the men were a raucous, boot-stomping group who immediately had the audience either clapping or dancing on the far end of the porch.

The woman, with her long flowing hair and a transcendent voice, accompanied herself on the mountain dulcimer, providing the audience with meditative, peaceful breaks. Sarah was again intrigued by the sounds emanating from this haunting instrument.

Sarah enjoyed the performances, particularly the woman's music as it helped to calm her jangled nerves. Although she was eager to hear from Charles and was worried about her friend, she would never forget this unique experience under the stars.

Chapter 9

It was the fifth day of the retreat and they were almost ready to put their rows together. Everyone had finished their pieced blocks, even the two women who did their own creations. Cheryl had passed out the packets of pictures and Sarah began spreading them out on her table. She was surprised at the quality and could hardly wait to tell Charles how they came out.

Brenda told them to begin figuring out where they wanted to place each of the photos. Sarah decided to put them in order with the actual ceremony in the top rows and their honeymoon pictures toward the bottom. Through the middle would be all the friends and family pictures.

The lavender in her Ohio Star blocks made Sophie's lavender dress stand out. Sophie was her matron of honor and Charles had picked up the color of her dress in his cummerbund. Both pictures looked excellent placed next to her colorful pieced blocks. Her daughter Martha was wearing an aqua suit, so her picture also looked nice against the aqua and lavender blocks.

Once she had her layout planned, Brenda told her to start putting borders around the photos to make them a consistent eight-and-a-half inches square to match the pieced blocks.

Once that was done, Sarah was comfortably on familiar turf. Sewing the rows together and adding the borders would be easy for her, whereas there were several new quilters who would need help.

Sarah kept her cell phone handy, hoping to hear from Charles. When he hadn't called by lunchtime, she decided to call him.

Standing on the front porch, she immediately got a dial tone.

"Hi, babe," he answered. "I was just sitting down in the backyard getting ready to call you. Would you believe I'm sitting here looking at Barney's nose which is sticking out of the doghouse where he's been all day?"

"He's inside the doghouse?"

"You bet. He's inside and apparently he loves it."

Barney opened one eye and looked at Charles. Then closed it again and sighed.

"Do you have news for me?" she asked, unable to wait for him to get around to telling her.

"I called the courthouse out there. Unfortunately, there's no record of a Higginbottom-Higginbottom divorce being filed in Las Vegas,"

"That's not good news."

"Then I tried finding the wife through information, Ballou and Higginbottom both. No luck. I even tried using my cop identification and checked for unlisted numbers."

"Still no luck?" Sarah asked.

"No luck. I talked to John and he's going to get his FBI friend involved in finding the woman, although we don't know much about her."

"I think I should let Sophie know what you're doing. It would be a relief to her to know someone is working on it. Higgy is still in a fog about the whole thing and doesn't know what to do. They're both terribly disappointed."

"Yeah, go ahead and tell her. I think I'll give Higgy a call tonight and see if I can drag more information out of him. Do you have his cell phone number?"

"Just call Sophie's cell." She also gave him Tim's house phone number in case he needed it. They went on to talk about what they'd been doing. Sarah described the photo blocks and her excitement with the way they came out.

That afternoon Sarah got her rows put together and laid the borders next to it to see how it was going to look. She was very pleased with the overall look and knew Charles would love it.

Sarah smiled as she cleaned up her area and went up to her room. She had decided to spend the evening reading and possibly calling her daughter, Martha.

Chapter 10

Sarah was surprised to find that her cell phone wasn't working at the overlook. It was about 10:00 the next morning, and she had taken a break in order to talk to Charles and find out what he learned from Higgy the night before. She had tried from the porch and there was no signal there. Other women at breakfast had said they were having trouble today. They were expecting a storm later in the day and they figured that was causing the interference. She had walked to the overlook, feeling comfortable now with that route through the woods, but there was no signal there either.

She was disappointed, but she stood for a while and marveled at the view. She decided to follow the edge of the precipice to the right and see if she could find a better spot. Following the curve of the ledge, she began to get another view of the valley, more to the right where a river snaked its way through the basin. She saw several trailers along the river banks. *What a peaceful place to live*, she mused, stopping to absorb the serene beauty.

No matter how far she continued, she never found a signal, so she decided to turn back. When she came to the trail, she turned left to return to the lodge. She noticed the path was somewhat overgrown in places and wondered why she hadn't noticed that before. She was aware of the tinkling of a shallow stream meandering through the rocks not far from the path. Suddenly she realized the path she was following was a dirt path, not the gravel nature trail she had followed to get up to the overlook. *I turned too soon*, she told herself.

Ahead, the dirt path was beginning to disappear into the woods. Not wanting to turn back, she continued following the path that was becoming less visible, but she had the feeling it was leading her toward the lodge. She stopped suddenly when she heard twigs snapping nearby followed by a rustling in the weeds to her left. She became tense and crouched in the thicket. *Am I being followed?* She could hear the rustling of the tall grasses along the edge of the stream. She could feel the tingle on the back of her neck as fear crept up her spine.

Whether she was being followed by a person or an animal, Sarah knew she had to get back to the lodge. She decided to take a leap of faith and cut straight through the woods toward what she thought would be the location of the original nature trail. She tried to run, but found herself restricted by her aging joints. She had a mental image of a younger version of herself running quickly through the woods, leaping over fallen trees. In fact, she was barely moving and when she came to fallen trees, she needed to stop and carefully step over them one foot at a time. *When did I get so old and stiff*, she asked herself, trying to take her attention off the potential danger.

When she spotted the nature trail straight ahead, she took a deep breath, feeling safe for a moment before realizing she still had a long way to go. Once she reached the path, she quickened her pace and headed toward the lodge.

Suddenly, and before she realized what was happening, her left ankle collapsed beneath her and she struggled to catch herself but fell to the ground with a gasp. She moaned and looked around feeling extremely vulnerable. Her ankle was throbbing and she hoped it wasn't broken. Wondering what had happened, she looked back at the trail and saw that there was a rutted area along the side of the path. She realized she must have stepped too close to the edge and lost her balance.

She started to get up but felt a stabbing pain in her ankle and decided to stay on the ground until she could evaluate whether she was seriously injured.

Suddenly, she froze. The tall grasses near her were parting. Something or someone was closely approaching her.

"You okay, lady?" A small boy crept out of the grasses and walked toward her holding out his hand as if to help her up.

"I just fell, but what are you doing out here?" she asked.

The boy dropped his hand and started to speak, but instead turned and ran through the grasses and out of sight.

The boy had appeared young, probably no more than seven or eight. His hair was long and disheveled, his clothes ripped and dirty. He was barefoot. Sarah stared after him in surprise. She listened for footsteps, wondering if he had been alone, but the woods were now silent.

Pulling herself together, she tried standing and found that, although in pain, she could walk. *I must have sprained my ankle*, she told herself, realizing the pain was familiar. She had turned her ankle often when she was attempting to learn to ice skate when she was young and twice it had been sprained. The instructor had told her she had weak ankles and needed to spend time building them up.

She thought about stopping and trying her cell phone again, *but who would I call*, she wondered. Charles couldn't help her and she didn't want to tell the people at the lodge she was lost in the woods. *But then I'm not lost*, she reassured herself. In fact, she was beginning to recognize the signs on the flora and knew she was moments away from the lodge.

When she burst out into the parking lot by the lodge, she saw several quilters from her group. They waved as if nothing had happened.

Has anything really happened? she asked herself. *I made a wrong turn. I heard sounds in the woods that could have easily been an animal, but was probably the young boy. I fell.* She shook her head, reprimanding herself for such histrionics. *This isn't like me at all*, she admonished herself.

* * * * *

The afternoon was spent working on their quilts. Peggy, a fellow quilter, had wrapped Sarah's ankle and agreed it was probably a sprain. Sarah refused a ride to the hospital, knowing it would be better in a few days. She was still a little shaky from her experience, but had told herself she was overreacting.

"Sarah, are you okay?" Holly asked.

"I'm still a little shaky from the fall, but I'm fine." She started to tell her about the boy, but thought better of it.

He probably lives up here in the mountains. She felt a strange loyalty toward him. He had obviously been concerned about her fall, but his desire to get away was stronger. She wondered if she would ever see him again.

By midafternoon, Sarah's ankle was throbbing. She had added her inner borders and one of the outer borders, but wasn't able to stand any longer. She realized her ankle was swelling and knew she needed to sit down and prop it up. She pulled a chair over and found a cushion she could place on it to raise her foot. While she was sitting, she took the opportunity to calculate the amount of fabric she would need for her quilt back but decided not to buy that until she returned home so she could get a coordinated fabric from the same line. The group was taking a field trip the next day to a quilt shop and several of the quilters had indicated they were going to buy backs for their quilts.

That evening the quilters were invited to a play. Holly had wrapped ice in a towel for her and, after a few hours of propping it up, the swelling had gone down and she was able to walk without undue pain. Despite Holly's objections, she decided to go to the play. "I'll just be sitting," she had assured Holly.

The play was being performed by a local high school; the young people were doing their interpretation of *The American Quilt*. Sarah had seen the movie with Winona Ryder and was eager to see how these kids would present it. Sarah loved live plays, and they didn't have to be professional actors. She enjoyed all plays and respected anyone willing to get up on the stage.

Coby again drove them, but there were only six quilters signed up so they took the minivan. As they pulled out of the parking lot, Sarah glanced toward the woods thinking about the boy; but later, enjoying the play, she put all thoughts aside of her experience in the woods and even of the young boy.

After the play, they stopped at a country store that had an ice cream machine, and they sat in the parking lot talking about the play. The general consensus was that the book was better than the movie, and that the play was, as one woman said, "Absolutely precious!"

It was late when they arrived back at the lodge, but even before they reached the final turn, they could see the bright lights. A police car had passed them on the country road as they were approaching. When they pulled in, they were surprised to see five or six police cars spread out around the parking lot. Spotlights were pointed toward the woods and two officers were standing by the entrance to the nature trail.

Cody parked out of the way on the far side of the lot and got out. He turned to the women as they were getting out of the van and said, "Wait here. I'll see what's going on." They watched him walk up to a policeman who was standing nearby and the two young men spoke for a few seconds. They saw Coby shake his head in disbelief.

When he returned to the van, his face was flushed and he simply said, "They want us to go in through the back door."

"What's going on," Sarah asked. Jane came up beside her to see what was happening.

Coby paused a moment, then said, "Some woman has disappeared from the lodge."

Jane turned pale and gasped, "Mama," as she ran toward the nearest policeman. He tried to direct her back to the van, but Sarah could tell she was arguing with him. He finally led her over to an official-looking man wearing a suit whom Sarah assumed was the lead detective. They talked and Sarah could see Jane was now crying.

It was her mother.

Chapter 11

As the sun was coming up, Sarah realized no one in the quilt group had been to bed. For most of the night, they had been huddled on the front porch watching as the police, aided by the Canine Unit, searched the woods. They had refused to allow the quilters to join in the search.

Sarah had spent most of the night attempting to keep Jane calm. "How could I have left her," she cried. "I never should have gone...."

"Jane, this isn't your fault." Sarah had brought Jane coffee and a cinnamon roll, both of which remained untouched. The staff had served breakfast inside and the group ate in shifts with two or three people staying with Jane and Sarah at all times.

"I thought she was sleeping," Mary Beth wailed. "I'm so sorry. I just went into the kitchen for a few minutes. I'm so-o-o sorry...."

The police questioned the evening staff on the desk and no one had seen her leave. "She might have slipped out the back door," one young man suggested. The search team revised their search area and began combing the woods behind the lodge as well.

Sarah asked Holly to sit with Jane while she walked around to the back. She'd been watching the activity in the front of the building for hours, and was curious about what was happening behind the lodge.

She headed down the front steps and one of the policemen looked her way but didn't stop her. She began walking around the lodge, staying close to the building. As she reached the dumpster, she heard a sound in the woods to her left. She stopped and listened, again feeling that tingle up her spine. *Something is always out there. . . . Watching? Waiting?*

Suddenly the tall grasses parted and two people stepped out holding hands. Genevieve, disheveled and dirty, was being led by the young barefoot boy. He looked pleadingly into Sarah's eyes. "Can you help her?" he said, handing the woman off to Sarah.

"Of course," she replied pulling Genevieve into her arms. The boy quickly turned toward the woods but stopped and looked back at Sarah. "Don't tell them about me. . . ." and he disappeared into the grasses.

* * * * *

Jane decided to take her mother and return home. Although her mother seemed to have enjoyed the adventure, Jane was exhausted from worry and guilt. Everyone congregated around the van later that morning to say goodbye and Genevieve held onto Sarah's hand and thanked her. She seemed to have forgotten about the boy who was the one who brought her home; Sarah was relieved because she, too, hadn't mentioned him. Again, she felt a kind of loyalty as if he were trusting her with a secret, but she had no idea what that secret was.

Coby drove off and the group met briefly in the quilting room. Brenda said they had canceled classes for the day but the room would remain open if anyone wanted to sew. She also offered to drive to the quilt shop in Gatlinburg but everyone agreed they only wanted to sleep.

By that time, Sarah's ankle was swollen and throbbing. Peggy told her to get an ice pack from the kitchen and put her foot up for a few hours and added that she'd re-wrap it after their naps. An exhausted group of quilters made their way up the stairs as Sarah stuck her head into the kitchen. Mary Beth saw her and hurried over. They talked for a few minutes, with the young woman continuing to apologize and Sarah attempting to explain to her the difficulty of caring for a person with dementia. "You did the best you could, Mary Beth. Just try to accept that and let it go. No one blames you."

Mary Beth brought her an ice bag and walked her to the elevator. "I didn't know this was here!" Sarah exclaimed, relieved that she didn't have to hobble up the stairs.

"I'll ride along with you."

When they got to Sarah's room, Mary Beth followed her in and helped her remove the bandage and get comfortable with her foot raised on pillows, which Mary Beth arranged for her. Sarah asked for her book and her cell phone and settled in for the afternoon.

When she woke up three hours later, the book and cell phone were exactly where Mary Beth had laid them. The ice bag was no longer cold, her foot had slipped off the pillows, and it was 3:30 in the afternoon. Sarah sat up and was pleased to notice that her ankle was feeling much better. It was hardly swollen and didn't hurt when she stepped on it.

She took a shower, ate an apple, and sat down to call Charles. Much had happened since they last talked, and she briefly wondered how much to tell him. She needn't have concerned herself about it, however.

"Sarah, am I ever glad you called. I have so much to tell you." He excitedly started telling Sarah about his search for Higgy's ex-wife. "The first problem was that we had the wrong name. She's not Lulu and never was. Lulu Ballou was just her stage name forty-some years ago."

"So what's her real name?" Sarah asked.

"Llewellyn. Llewellyn Ballard. She married a Ralph Ballard thirty-five years ago, and they have three children and eight grandchildren."

"That's good news! That means she got a divorce, right?"

"Wrong."

"Wrong? Then how did she get married to this Ballard fellow?"

"That's the fun part. She told me her marriage to Higgy *didn't count*."

"What?" Sarah shrieked. "Are you kidding me?"

"I'm dead serious. Just listen to the explanation. The justice of the peace who supposedly married them collected $200 cash for the privilege, and that was a tidy sum forty years ago!" Charles added as an aside.

"Go on, Charles. Please. Why didn't the marriage count?"

"Okay, so he performed the ceremony, but, in fact, he was never licensed to perform marriages at all! Our friend Higgy wasn't the only one who got duped by the good Justice Jeremiah Brown. He performed dozens of marriages that year—and, as Higginbottom told us, none of them count."

"Did Higgy know that? Is that why he said it didn't count?"

"Nope. He had no idea. He just lucked out. Ironic isn't it? Higgy said it didn't count … and sure enough it didn't, but for entirely different reasons."

"Hmm," Sarah responded, not wanting to put words to her thoughts about this man her dear friend was planning to marry. "So he's not married and he's free to marry Sophie?"

"He's free to marry her. Whether or not she'll marry him is yet to be determined," Charles responded.

"Did you talk to her?" Sarah asked, surprised by his response.

"No, but I talked to Higgy. He said she currently isn't speaking to him and she sent him packing."

"What does that mean?" Sarah asked.

"He's been moved, bag and baggage, to the local hotel."

"Oh my. I've got to talk to Sophie. I'm surprised she hasn't called me."

"She may have tried. I haven't been able to reach you for the past two days. You must have a very weak signal up there."

"We've had problems with that," Sarah responded. "I think I'll call her now. It's about noon there now, I guess."

"I miss you," Charles said after a short pause. "I really miss you. Ten days is too long to be apart."

"I know. I miss you too. I have some things I want to talk over with you, but not just now. I'll try to call later."

"Are you okay?" he asked sounding very concerned.

"It's nothing to worry about. I just wanted to talk a few things over with you. Talking with you always helps me get clarity."

"Okay, sweetheart. I'll wait to hear from you when you're ready." They hung up reluctantly.

Ten days is indeed too long to be apart, she thought as she dressed to go downstairs.

Chapter 12

The excitement the previous day had everyone on edge, and Brenda asked if the group would like to cancel the remaining three days of the retreat. Two women thought it would be a good idea, but the rest wanted to stay, so it was decided to continue the retreat. Most of the quilters had completed their memory quilts. Sarah had finished hers the previous evening after her nap.

The next project was a surprise to the group. Cheryl passed out sketching paper and pencils and told the group to design a wall hanging that they would be making as a reminder of the retreat. They were told they could do anything they wanted to do. Several of the women looked around with confused looks on their faces as if they had no idea where to start. A few others started right in sketching. Sarah didn't start sketching right away, but her head was spinning with ideas: trees, mountains, autumn colors. She had no idea how she would translate these ideas into a wall hanging, but she was excited about the project.

Meanwhile, Brenda came into the room carrying a large basket of scraps and told the group they were welcome to use their own fabric or anything they wanted from the scrap basket.

"I have extra fabric too," Peggy announced and others joined in saying they also had extra they could contribute to the scrap basket. At this point, the basket was overflowing.

"Also," Brenda added returning to the room with a box of fat quarters, "the quilt shop in Gatlinburg donated these fat quarters for our projects. ..."

"We missed our field trip to their shop," one of the retreaters said. "Will there be another chance to go?"

"We're going to offer several optional activities on the last day. One will be to go into Gatlinburg if anyone is interested. I'll have the schedule tomorrow."

Looking through the fabrics, an idea was beginning to take shape in Sarah's head. "I'll be right back," she announced as she hurried toward the door. She was remembering an evening the previous week when she was sitting on the porch late at night marveling at the size of the harvest moon hanging proudly over the mountain range in the distance.

And that memory was bringing to mind something from the museum. She had picked up brochures and she thought there was a picture of it there. She hurried to her room and opened the brochures and within seconds was looking at the Moon Over the Mountain quilt block. *Perfect!* She thought. *This is what I'll make to remember this experience forever.*

Sarah quickly scanned through her fabrics looking for anything that looked like a mountain, a sky, or a moon.

She was disappointed to find that her flowery fabrics just weren't right.

She sat down to think about it and immediately pictured the batiks Teresa had discarded since she didn't think they would look right in her memory quilt.

Sarah hurried back to the classroom with her brochure, almost forgetting about her ankle. As she approached the staircase, a twinge in her ankle reminded her to use the elevator.

Once back in the classroom, Sarah was pleased to see that everyone was milling around talking and picking through the fabrics. She went directly to Teresa and asked about the batik scraps. "I have them right here," she said reaching for her tote bag. "Help yourself to whatever you want; I was getting ready to donate them to the scrap basket." Sarah spread them out and found several which could be used for the mountain. She couldn't decide which would be best, but then realized she could use them all by cutting them into strips. At first, she couldn't find a moon, but then a beautiful piece of autumn gold seemed to be calling to her, and she suddenly remembered it had been a harvest moon. "I love it!" she said aloud as she added it to her batch of scraps.

She then headed for the basket and Holly joined her. "What are you looking for?" she asked and Sarah told her about her idea.

"What I need is a night sky."

They found several blues and even one with white that could be clouds. Holly pulled out a multicolored batik in bright colors and said that it could be a sky at sunset. But none seemed quite right.

I need a night sky, Sarah reminded herself. Then she saw it. It was tucked in the bottom of the basket and was a mottled black and blue batik. "Perfect," she exclaimed as she pulled the piece from the basket and determined there was at least a half-yard.

An hour later, three women were still rummaging through the basket looking for fabric and several were still working on their sketches. Cheryl and Brenda were helping the ones who were having trouble getting started, but Sarah was working full steam ahead. "I'll be right back," she announced again and hurried to the kitchen. "Mary Beth," she called out, "I need a saucer."

"A saucer? Do you need a cup too?"

"No, just a saucer, but I could also use a piece of freezer paper if you have any."

She returned with the saucer and freezer paper, and she used the saucer to make a pattern and then cut a large harvest moon from the beautiful gold fabric. "I love it," she said, standing back to admire her handiwork.

Turning to Holly, Sarah said, "I just realized I'll have to appliqué these pieces on."

"Sure, but why don't you machine appliqué them."

"Good idea, but I've never done that." Sarah noticed that Cheryl didn't seem to be occupied, so she asked her if she would show her how.

"I'd be happy to. In fact, two other quilters have asked about that, so let's have a short demonstration right after lunch." She turned to the class and told them about it. She then added, "It's a beautiful afternoon and perfect for a nature hike or curling up in a lounge chair on the porch, so let's end class at 3:00 today."

"What about our wall hangings," one of the quilters asked, looking worried.

Knowing that most of the class would be finished by 3:00, Cheryl offered to leave the classroom open for anyone who wanted to continue sewing.

* * * * *

Sarah headed for the porch with her cell phone hoping to reach Sophie. Again, she couldn't get a signal so she decided to venture out toward the overlook. Her ankle was feeling better, although Peggy told her to keep it wrapped for another few days.

As she strolled down the trail, she listened to the sounds of nature: small animals and birds flitting about, a gentle breeze through the leaves, an occasional bird calling to its mate, … *absolutely nothing for me to fear*, she reminded herself. A squirrel scampered up a tree and out the limb hanging across the path. He stopped and looked at her before scurrying on. Sarah smiled to herself and wondered how she could have been so frightened. She thought about how one's mind can play tricks. Once she reached the overlook, she sat down on a flattened boulder and dialed Sophie's cell phone.

"Hi, kiddo," Sophie said as she answered on the first ring. "I was hoping you'd call today." They talked about what Charles had learned, and Sophie told Sarah she was fed up with Higgy. "He just sat around with his head in his hands saying 'What am I going to do?' and he proceeded to do absolutely nothing! He left it all up to Charles. I just wonder, Sarah. Do I want to spend the rest of my days with this man? He's still talking about getting married next week."

"Maybe you need more time, Sophie."

"I know. I think I'll tell him I want to wait until after Christmas. Timmy would be home and I'd have you as my matron of honor, assuming there's a wedding at all. That's better I think. Don't you?"

"I do, Sophie. I think you need time to be sure this is what you want. When do you think you'll be coming home?"

"I want to spend another week with Timmy. I might let Higgy come back to Timmy's house. I guess Charles told you …?"

"Yes, about the hotel. I was sorry you had all that to go through, but I had to laugh when Charles told me you threw him out 'bag and baggage.' "

Sophie chuckled. "Yeah. I sort of overdid it. I'll call and see if he wants to come back. He's probably more comfortable over there actually. I took the guest room when we got here and Timmy set up a rollaway bed in his room for Higgy. With his back problems, he probably was glad to get into a good bed at the hotel. Anyway, I'll ask him."

After they hung up, Sarah sighed. She was glad she and Charles had worked out their issues and were settled into married life. She knew Sophie had lots of thinking to do over the next few months.

She continued to sit on the boulder in the sunshine. She was now enjoying the sounds of the forest and sat with her eyes closed and the sun on her face.

"Hi, lady."

Sarah jumped up and her cell phone fell to the ground shattering. The boy jumped back, his eyes wide open with surprise.

"Oh," she said once she realized it was the boy. "I'm sorry. I didn't mean to frighten you. I was just surprised."

"It's okay." He bent over and began picking up the pieces of her cell phone. "It's broke," he said as he handed the pieces to her.

"Let's see if we can put it back together," she suggested, thinking that might keep him with her for a few minutes. She spread the pieces out and was immediately aware that once the back of the case was put on, the phone was probably in working order. The other pieces were only cosmetic, but she didn't say anything about that to the boy. "Where shall we start?" she asked.

He picked up the basic two pieces and set them on the boulder. He took the batteries and slipped them into their grooves. "Thar," he muttered as he snapped the case together. Reaching for the other pieces, he quickly snapped them into place and handed it to Sarah.

"Thank you," Sarah said enthusiastically. "I'm Sarah. What's your name?"

The boy hesitated but finally said, "Ma called me 'Boy,' but I'm Richard, like my Paw, 'cept they call me Ricky."

"Do you live around here?" Sarah asked, hoping not to scare him away like before.

Again he hesitated but seemed to decide to respond. "Yea," he said simply without elaborating. Sarah decided not to pursue it. He seemed to be getting nervous so she decided not to ask him any more questions.

"It's pretty out there," she said, looking out over the valley.

"Yea, ... long way down," he responded.

I wonder if he lives down there. "I wish I could climb down there," she commented hoping to get more out of him. "Do you think I could make it?"

The boy smiled. "I don't think so," he responded. After a few long pause, he added, "I fall sometimes."

Now she knew he climbs up and down the valley wall and she wondered if he lived in one of the shacks along the river below. "I'd like to go down to one of those houses," pointing toward the river.

"Why?" the boy asked looking guarded.

"Oh, just to visit ... maybe have a cup of tea and say hello."

Frowning, the boy said, "Addie May ain't got no tea."

"I could bring tea," she responded casually continuing to look out over the valley and wondering who Addie May was, but didn't ask. "Maybe even cookies," she added, watching the boy's reaction out of the side of her eye.

The boy didn't respond but was studying her carefully. A few minutes later, he turned toward the woods, and said, "Gotta git home," and he was gone.

Sarah sat for a while thinking about the young boy named Richard-like-his-Paw. He was barefoot as usual, his clothes were soiled, and he was in dire need of a good scrubbing. She wondered who takes care of him. She thought he had used the past tense when he referred to his mother, but wasn't sure.

She had so many questions. *Who is this boy?*, she wondered. *And is this who's been watching me?* All she knew about him was that he was cautious and secretive, but also gentle and kind. *So young*, she thought sadly. *So very young.* She wanted to know his story and hoped she would have the chance.

Chapter 13

Sarah's wall hanging was complete and displayed in the classroom. After a few false starts, she caught onto the machine appliquéing technique and was pleased with the final result. She took a picture of it with her cell phone and sent it to Charles. Her quilt top was finished and her binding was made. The only thing left was to buy the back when she got home and have it quilted.

The next day would be the last day of the retreat and several activities were being offered. Brenda was taking the minivan into Gatlinburg for anyone interested in sightseeing, souvenir shopping, or spending time at the fabric shop they had missed earlier in the week when Genevieve was missing.

Coby was offering a bus trip across the Great Smoky Mountains National Park, stopping at Clingman's Dome for those willing to hike. "It's the highest point in Tennessee," Brenda had said, "and not for the faint-hearted, but it's a spectacular view." She explained that the lodge was providing a bag lunch for anyone interested and requested that the quilters sign up today so the lodge will know how many lunches to prepare.

Cheryl stood up and added, "Some of you haven't finished your projects, and I'll be here for anyone who needs help and wants to stay behind tomorrow."

Sarah wasn't sure what to do. She was reluctant to sign up for a trip since she hoped to see young Ricky again. She didn't know what it was, but something about him left her feeling that she was needed in some way.

In the end, she decided to sign up for the trip through the park. If she didn't go, she could always pick up the bag lunch and eat it in the lodge's picnic area.

* * * * *

It was early evening and Sarah was strolling around the grounds enjoying the beauty of the mountain ridges and realizing that her retreat was about to come to an end. The sun was setting and the sky was aflame with brilliant shades of red, orange, and yellow. She sat on a rustic bench that had been placed facing the setting sun. She wished Charles was by her side enjoying this miraculous sight.

At dusk, she stood and headed back to the lodge. As she was approaching, she heard voices coming from the side door. She could make out two figures: a woman and a small child. At first she assumed it was Mary Beth and her sister, but then she remembered seeing Sissy leaving with Coby earlier. She walked closer and could see it was, in fact, Mary Beth and she was talking to a child. *The boy?* Sarah moved closer.

As she approached, it was clearly Ricky standing at the back door as Mary Beth handed him a large parcel. Sarah stepped into the shadows and watched curiously. A moment later, a car pulled up and the boy hurried to the passenger's side and got in. As the car sped off, Sarah recognized it as Coby's car, the same car that had left earlier with Sissy. *What's going on?* She asked herself, completely baffled by this turn of events.

Once inside the building, Sarah headed for the kitchen door and pushed it open. No one was there except Mary Beth who was putting the last of the clean dishes into the serving rack. She looked surprised when she looked up and saw Sarah.

"Sorry to startle you," Sarah said. "I'm wondering if you have a few minutes? I'd like to talk with you."

Mary Beth looked around nervously and asked, "Have I done something wrong?"

"Oh no, Mary Beth. I'm just hoping you can help me with something."

"Of course," the young girl responded with a relieved smile. "I'm just finishing up here. Would you like me to come to your room?"

"That's a good idea. I'll see you upstairs whenever you're free."

A few minutes later there was a meek knock at her door. Sarah greeted Mary Beth and offered her a seat by the open window. There was a gentle breeze moving the lace curtains ever so slightly. The evening air smelled fresh and clean.

"What did you want me to help you with, Mrs. Parker?" Mary Beth asked.

"It's the young boy, Ricky."

Suddenly Mary Beth looked frightened, and her eyes darted around as if she were seeking an escape.

"Mary Beth, it's nothing to worry about. I just met the boy on the trail and he looks like he needs some sort of help.

I saw you talking with him, and I was hoping you could tell me if there's anything I can do."

She saw Mary Beth begin to relax. The girl looked directly at Sarah before she spoke, took a deep breath, and finally said, "He needs help, but I don't know if there's anything you can do."

"Tell me about it, Mary Beth. I might be able to help."

"Well, his mama died in childbirth a couple of years ago, and his dad is raising the kids alone. At least he was up until a few months ago."

Sarah saw that Mary Beth's eyes were filling with tears and she handed her a box of tissues. She wanted to ask questions, but decided to remain quiet and let the young girl tell the story. After she blotted her eyes, Mary Beth continued. "They were doing okay until he lost his job when the mill closed last year. He was out of work for a long time. He finally got a job, but it wasn't close by. Addie May, that's the oldest one, thinks he's doing strip mining up in West Virginia somewhere. He was gone all week but came home every Friday night and took care of the family until really early in the morning on Monday when he left for work again. He always brought a week's worth of food and some money when he came home."

"Where do they live?"

"Down yonder in the holler," Mary Beth responded. "Not far as the crow flies and about a mile by road. Coby drives me over sometimes."

Sarah noticed Mary Beth was lapsing into mountain vernacular and she smiled to herself, knowing that the girl was beginning to feel more comfortable.

"It's pretty rundown," Mary Beth continued, "There are four kids: the baby, she's almost three, I guess; a boy around six; Ricky who's eight; and there's a thirteen-year-old girl. She's holding the family together by herself."

"The thirteen-year-old? But you said the father's there weekends, right?" Sarah still wasn't clear just what the problem was.

"He doesn't do that anymore."

"What?" Sarah responded thinking she must have misunderstood. "He doesn't come home weekends anymore?"

"No. A couple of months ago he just didn't show up. They don't know why. After a while they ran out of money and food. That's when I met Ricky. I caught him taking food out of the dumpster. He was scared when I caught him, but I told him it was okay. He came every day and after a while I started packing leftovers for him to take home. Sometimes Coby drives him home. It's really a sad situation."

"Can't the county do something to help them?" Sarah asked and was surprised to see Mary Beth's shocked reaction.

"No, Mrs. Parker," she pleaded. "Please don't turn them in. The county will separate them and send them Lord knows where. They'll be okay until their dad comes back. He mustn't come home and find them gone. He loves those kids more than anything."

"Then why isn't he there with them?" Sarah asked, sounding very judgmental and was immediately sorry. She could see Mary Beth withdraw. "I'm sorry, Mary Beth. Of course, he loves them, and I'm sure he'd be here if he could. Something must have happened to keep him away."

The two continued to talk for another half-hour until Mary Beth looked at the clock and reached for her jacket. "Coby's waiting to drive me home," she said.

"I'd like to go to their house," Sarah said as she stood and walked the girl to the door. "Do you think that's possible?"

"I think so. Ricky seems to trust you," Mary Beth responded. "We'll talk more tomorrow." With a quick hug, Sarah promised to do everything she could to find some way to help the children.

After Mary Beth left, Sarah tried her cell phone but there was no signal. The lodge switchboard was closed for the night and she thought about heading out toward the overlook, but immediately dismissed the idea. "I'll call Charles first thing in the morning," she told herself aloud as she headed for the shower.

Her sleep was disturbed by dreams of young barefoot children running loose in the mountains.

Chapter 14

"Charles. I'm so glad you're up. I need to talk to you." It was early morning and Sarah had been pleased to see that she had a strong signal and could call from her own room.

"You sound upset, sweetie. What's going on?"

Sarah could imagine him moving to the nearest chair and sitting down to give her his full attention. He always did that when someone wanted to speak with him, whether on the telephone or in person. There was never any question that he was listening. In fact, as a detective he had perfected the skill of listening to the words, the body language, and especially the things not said.

Sarah took a deep breath and began. She told him about the movements in the woods the night she arrived and her experiences on the nature trail. Then she told him about the boy, how he came to help her when she fell. ...

"You fell?" he interrupted with a voice filled with anxiety and concern.

"It was nothing, Charles. I just turned my ankle. I'm fine now ... and that's not the point." She went on with her story, telling him about the night Genevieve wandered off and about the massive police search. She knew this was another point he wanted to interrupt, but he managed to hold back. She told him about Ricky leading Genevieve out of the woods, about him getting leftovers from the lodge, and about the things she learned from talking with Mary Beth. "I'm worried about the children, Charles. I want to help, but I don't want to cause trouble for them. Mary Beth said they are afraid the county will come in and separate them."

Charles sat quietly for a few moments, then asked, "Do you think the father just ran off?"

"I don't think so, Charles. Everything I hear about him is good. He was nearly destroyed by the death of his wife, but Mary Beth says he threw himself into caring for the children. Her father went to school with Richard, that's the father, and Mary Beth grew up around him. Her family thinks the world of him."

Again, Charles remained quiet for a few moments, then said, "I think the best way we can help the family is to find the father. Does Mary Beth have any ideas?"

"No, just that he was working somewhere in West Virginia doing strip mining. Maybe Mary Beth's father knows exactly where. I'll have her ask him." There was a long pause before Sarah said, "I want to go to the house, but I don't want to be seen as interfering. I'm hoping I can get Ricky to invite me."

"How would you get there?"

"I think Coby would take me. ..."

"Coby?"

"He's Mary Beth's brother. He drives for the lodge. He brought us here from Knoxville last week."

Charles remained very quiet. Sarah wondered what was going through his mind, but didn't ask, knowing that he needed time to think a situation through. Finally he spoke saying, "Do you think you can keep your room at the lodge for a few days?"

"I'm sure I can, but …"

"I'm thinking about coming there and helping you with this. There's a good chance I can make some headway toward finding out what's happened to the father. I'll have to get the police involved. …"

"No Charles. I promised I wouldn't do anything that could lead to the county coming in and taking the kids away."

"Sarah, they may not be safe there in the long run, but okay, I'll try to find the father on my own. …" He paused again, but then added, "Sarah, we might have to involve the authorities at some point. They're just kids. …"

"I know, Charles. I know.

* * * * *

The van was ready to leave for Gatlinburg and Sarah was still ambivalent. She wanted to see the town, but didn't want to miss an opportunity to talk to Ricky. With Charles planning to come the next day, she needed to make sure the family was going to accept their help. She waved the van away and turned to return to the lodge when she saw Mary Beth hurrying toward her.

"I talked to Addie May about you going over to see them," she said. Coby had taken his sister to the Abernathy house early that morning so she could talk with all the kids. Addie May, Mary Beth had explained, was very reluctant, fearing it could cause the county to come out, but Ricky had

argued on Sarah's behalf. "He trusts you, and I assured them you wouldn't contact the county."

Sarah felt a twinge of guilt, remembering what Charles had said. They would have to contact the authorities if the children weren't safe. She knew she might not be able to keep that promise, but she prayed they could find the father.

"Okay, so what happens next?" Sarah asked.

"Coby will drive you over there this afternoon. Are you leaving tomorrow?" Sarah told her about her husband coming and their plan to stay on a few days. She didn't mention that he was a retired police detective. On the one hand, that information could be encouraging—they stood a better chance of finding the missing father with a detective on the case. But, Sarah feared, they could also become mistrustful and not let them get involved at all.

"In that case," Mary Beth added, "let's wait until morning. We have lots of retreat activities going on here this evening, and I'd really like to go with you if that's okay with you. I think it would make things easier."

"I agree. Let's plan it for early tomorrow. I don't know when Charles will be arriving, but I think this first visit should be just you and me."

"Coby is making several trips into Knoxville tomorrow taking folks to the airport. Maybe he can pick your husband up as well."

"That would be terrific! I'll let you know his schedule just as soon as I get it."

Sarah walked up to her room feeling good. The pieces were falling into place, she was thinking. But suddenly she realized that none of their plans ensured the father would be found. In fact, all they had accomplished was getting

permission to visit the children. *We have a long way to go,* she told herself as she arrived back at her room.

"Are you going to the park?" Holly asked when Sarah answered the door a few minutes later. "I've decided to hike up to the dome."

"Really?" Sarah scanned through her mind and determined there was nothing she needed to do the rest of the day except find out when Charles would be arriving and she'd have her cell phone with her. "Why not!" She quickly changed her shoes and grabbed her purse and the two women hurried out to the parking lot where the bus was loading. As she got on, Coby smiled at her and quietly said, "Thanks for helping."

"What's that all about?" Holly asked as they were choosing a seat toward the back. Not wanting to tell anyone her plans, she just shrugged and starting talking about the cocktail party and farewell dinner the lodge had planned for the retreaters that evening.

"We'll be driving through the park for about an hour," Coby announced over his microphone once they were on the road. "We'll be stopping at a few overlooks and we'll get to Clingman's Dome around noon. There's a picnic area right there and I'll pass out the lunches. You can decide if you want to hike on up to the observation tower after lunch. For the ones that don't go, I'll drive around for a while and show you a few other attractions. We'll get back to the dome around 2:00 to pick up the hikers."

"How's the hike?" one of the quilters in the front of the bus asked.

"Well, it's only a half-mile hike, but it's all uphill and a fairly difficult walk at this altitude unless you're in pretty

good shape. Of course, there're benches along the way so you can rest. You can even turn around and come back; it's downhill coming back, you know," he added with a grin.

They rode slowly down the park road through forests and past peaceful streams and gentle waterfalls. Occasionally a curve in the road would bring them to an overlook high above a spectacular view of a valley with seemingly endless layers of blue mountain ridges beyond. As he drove, Coby gave them the history of the park and some interesting information about the wildlife and vegetation.

Sarah felt a tingle up her spine again when he talked about the wildlife. "These mountains are home to elk, coyote, bobcats, and black bears," Coby told the group. Sarah pictured herself walking along the meandering nature trail and hearing snapping noises in the brush which sounded like someone following her. For the last few days she had put her fears aside, assuming it had been the boy. Now she realized she actually could have been in real danger.

"… and twenty-seven species of rodents," Coby added and Sarah shuddered.

But she put all those thoughts behind her when the bus stopped and she looked out over a lush green valley hemmed in by sandstone cliffs and endless blue ridges as far as she could see.

As promised, the drive through the park had been spectacular. Sarah wished for Charles to be able to experience it first hand and hoped they could find time to drive through the park while he was there.

Maybe he should rent a car at the airport, she thought, realizing they would need to be able to get around.

After walking through Clingman's Dome Visitor Center and picking up a couple of souvenirs, Sarah and Holly shared a picnic table with several other women who planned to follow the trail up to the observation tower. Eager to start the hike, they crumpled their lunch bags and headed for the trail.

When Sarah first agreed to hike to the dome, she had completely forgotten about her ankle. She hadn't gone far up the paved trail before it started to throb, but she was determined to continue. *I can always stop and sit on a bench*, she assured herself, but in fact she was able to walk the entire way.

It was, indeed, a very steep incline.

As they reached the concrete walkway that curved high above the mountainside on its way up and out to the observation tower, Sarah leaned against the railing to rest, but the view immediately captured her attention. She just stood, overcome by the beauty of the rolling tree-covered mountains and valleys that blended into the horizon. A soft mist lay over the peaks in the far distance. "Spectacular," she said almost in a whisper as if her voice might disturb the tranquility.

Holly had brought a jacket and was buttoning it when Sarah turned around. "I wish I'd thought of that," she commented. There was a strong wind and it was much cooler as they approached the deck of the circular observation tower perched high above the sloping mountain. There was a sign indicating that the elevation was 6,643 feet.

They slowly walked around the circular tower, taking full advantage of the panoramic view. Not wanting to leave this magnificent spot, they stood by the rail until they realized

a crowd was forming behind them. Looking down the trail, they could see several busloads of people on their way up.

Once they got back to the lodge, Sarah was exhausted and in need of a shower and some time spent with her feet up. She put a call into Peggy's room to see if she would be willing to wrap her ankle again since it was swollen and painful.

After a few hours of rest, the quilters began to congregate in a private banquet room that had been set up with wine and cheese along with an array of hors d'oeuvres. Their projects, which had been collected earlier, were displayed around the room for everyone to admire.

Drew Harper, Holly's husband, had returned from his hike along the Appalachian Trail and was now the only man in the room. He seemed to be enjoying his exclusive position as a group of woman crowded around him. Walking closer to see what was going on, Sarah realized he was describing in detail his encounter with a black bear along the trail. "He probably spotted it a half-mile off the trail down in the valley," Holly whispered with a loving sparkle in her eye. "He loves attention."

After dinner, Sarah sat on the front porch, listening to the sounds of the forest and wondering what the next few days would bring. The food had been delicious, and the camaraderie with the quilters was very emotional as they realized their retreat had come to an end.

* * * * *

It took Sarah a moment to realize her cell phone was ringing. She glanced at the clock and saw it was 2:30 in the morning. She picked up the phone and squinted to read who was calling. "Sophie?" she said into the receiver, still feeling groggy.

"Oh no!" Sophie suddenly exclaimed. "I forgot about the time difference. Were you asleep?"

Shaking herself awake, Sarah responded as kindly as she could, "That's okay, Sophie." She clicked on the bedside lamp and arranged her pillows so she could sit up. "What's going on?"

"I'm flying home tomorrow," Sophie responded.

"You and Higgy are cutting your trip short?" Sarah responded, yawning and hoping her good friend would get to the point of her call quickly.

"No, I'm flying back alone."

"What about Higgy?" Sarah asked suddenly attentive.

"He left this morning for Las Vegas."

Chapter 15

Mary Beth stopped by Sarah's room early the next morning to let her know that Coby would drive them to the Abernathy home at 10:00.

Sarah hurried through her shower, went downstairs to pick up coffee and a breakfast sandwich, and returned to her room to call Charles. She figured he'd be up since he was flying to Tennessee later in the day.

"Hi, sweetie," he answered sounding sleepy.

"Did I wake you?" she asked apologetically.

"No, I just got off the phone with the airlines. I'll be arriving in Knoxville at 6:20 and should get to the lodge before 8:00. Will your friend Coby be able to meet me?"

"Charles, I think you should rent a car. We need to be able to get around without imposing on Coby, don't you think?"

"I agree. Good idea."

Sarah gave him the address and phone number. "Be sure you get a car with a GPS."

"I think they all have them now, but I'll bring my own just in case. What's your plan today?"

"Mary Beth and I are going to the Abernathy home so I can meet the kids and let them know you're coming to help find their father. Mary Beth has already talked to them, so it's not going to be a problem. I just wanted them to meet us one at a time since they don't see strangers often."

They went on to talk about how to approach their first visits when Sarah suddenly stopped and said, "Charles, I have something to tell you."

"Sounds serious. What is it, hon?"

"It's Sophie." Sarah told him about her conversation with Sophie the night before. "She realized they just weren't right for each other. She's glad they went to Alaska because it helped her see the problems. Tim helped too."

"Tim doesn't like him?"

"Well, Tim looks at him in terms of what he would like for his mother, and he feels Higgy just doesn't fit the bill."

"His buffoon-ness?"

Sarah laughed. "Yes, I guess it's partly that. But even I was taken by him at first. . . ."

"Oh?" Charles responded trying to pretend jealous outrage.

"Not that way, you silly man. I was taken in by the belief that he was good for Sophie. He was attentive and seemed to adore her, but …"

"But that isn't enough," Charles said, completing her sentence.

"No. They need to be compatible in the long run. Sophie is delightful. She has a great sense of humor and she's smart. She's friendly and outgoing. And Higgy … well, Higgy's …"

"A buffoon?"

"Okay, a buffoon," Sarah chuckled. "I just can't see her being happy with him in the long run. I know he'd be good to her; I just think she deserves more than that. Anyway, it doesn't matter what we think. She's decided not to marry him."

"Ah," he responded in a noncommittal tone, not wanting to admit that he was glad to hear Sophie had made what he considered to be the right decision. "And how did he take this?"

"He pleaded his case, of course, but once he was sure she meant it, he packed up and left for Las Vegas."

"Las Vegas?" Charles exclaimed with surprise. "Why Las Vegas?"

"To see Lulu," Sarah responded.

"What? Llewellyn Ballard?" he responded with surprise. "Why?"

"After you told him about her, he called and they talked for hours. She told him she and her husband had been separated for the past year...."

"I didn't know that," he responded surprised that she hadn't told him.

"Her divorce was final last week, and once he was sure Sophie wasn't going to marry him, he decided to go see her."

"Wow! That surprises me. I feel sort of sorry for the guy. I'm not sure what he's getting himself into."

"Well, he's not our problem now," Sarah said.

"Is Sophie staying up there with her son for a while?"

"No, she's flying home today. I was hoping you could pick her up, but you two will be crossing paths."

"That's right, they left Higgy's new SUV at her house. Call her and get her schedule, and tell her I'll arrange for someone to pick her up."

"Who?"

"Someone from the department. They have some new recruits that just started. They'll get a kick out of doing a favor for one of the old-timers."

"You do have a reputation there, don't you?" she responded with a chuckle. "I'm just glad you're *my* old-timer. I'll see you tonight."

Mary Beth tapped on the door, as she was hanging up. "Are you ready to go?"

* * * * *

The gray weathered clapboard house was run down and in dire need of repair, but Sarah could see that it had been someone's treasured home at some time in the past. The front porch was sagging, and the step leading up to it was askew, but there was latticework enclosing the space below the porch and a built-in planter on the exposed side of the covered porch. Two additions had obviously been added, a small one facing the front of the house and a two-story one on the back, probably bedrooms.

"Someone loved this house," Sarah said softly, not realizing she had spoken her thoughts aloud.

"The grandparents. Clara's parents," Mary Beth clarified. "Richard and Clara moved into her parent's house when they got married. Richard built on the addition for the parents and after they died, Clara and Richard's children filled up that part of the house."

"You said you visited here when you were young," Sarah said, hoping Mary Beth would share some of her memories.

"Our grandfather was good friends with Clara's parents and he used to bring Coby and me over here to play when we were kids. Clara was much older than we were, but she still played with us. That was before she married Richard, of course."

"And later your father became good friends with Richard?"

"Yes," Mary Beth replied. "Our families have been close for years."

Sarah spotted a well with an old-fashioned pump near the side door. A slanting gutter had been jerry-rigged at the roofline to carry rainwater to a barrel near the well. Realizing Sarah was looking up at it, Mary Beth explained, "Our grandfather built that. It's an awful looking thing, but it works." She smiled as she remembered running through the cornfield with Coby that day while the men worked on the contraption. "Clara's mama really fussed when she saw it," Mary Beth said with a chuckle.

Sarah noticed a utility pole with low slung wires running into the house and was glad to see the children had electricity.

"It's time for you two to hop out," Coby announced. "I've got to get back to the lodge. I'll be back for you in an hour. ..."

"Oh?" Sarah responded, looking disappointed. "I was hoping to spend some time with the children. ..."

"He's just coming to pick me up then," Mary Beth explained. "I need to get back to work, but if things are going well with you and the kids, you can stay longer. Coby can pick you up after his next trip to Knoxville."

"That sounds good, assuming the children want me to stay. I was hoping to do some cooking," she said as she reached into the back seat for the box of groceries she had asked Coby to pick up for her.

"I'll carry that," Mary Beth offered, taking the box from Sarah. As she was getting out of the car, Sarah handed Coby a slip of paper with her cell phone number and said, "Call me when you have an idea when you want to pick me up."

Coby nodded and handed Sarah his card as well saying, "And you call me if you need me sooner."

They waved to Coby as he drove away. Approaching the house, Sarah began to feel apprehensive, not knowing what to expect.

Before they had a chance to knock, the door was opened by a blond, curly-headed little girl. Looking at Sarah, she ran back and hid her face behind an older girl who Sarah assumed to be Addie May, the thirteen-year-old. Addie May smiled, and said, "That's Baby Girl. She's shy at first, but she won't be for long." Addie May tussled the little girl's curls and said, "Ain't that right, Baby Girl?"

The child put her thumb in her mouth but couldn't hold back the smile that spread across her face. She reached down and picked up a ragged cloth which Sarah assumed to be her security blanket, or what was left of it.

"I'm Addie May Abernathy," the older girl said attempting to look very grown up but was clearly very young to have all the responsibilities Sarah knew she had.

"Glad to meet you, Addie May." Looking down at the little girl, she added, "And I'm glad to meet you too." The little girl hid her face in the blanket.

"Nice to meet you, Miss Sarah," Addie May continued, "and that's my brother, Tommy, over there behind the chair. Tommy's six. You know Ricky already. I don't know where he got to," she added looking around the sparsely decorated room as if he might appear somewhere in the room.

Sarah knew Addie May was uneasy despite her attempts to appear in control. She hoped she could find a way to put the young girl's fears at ease, knowing she was afraid Sarah's visit would somehow trigger an investigation by the county.

"I hope you won't mind, but I brought along some food. I was hoping you and I could do some cooking together," Sarah said to Addie May as she started unpacking the box. The previous day, she had asked Coby to buy a large package of beef and bags of onions, potatoes, and carrots. "Do you kids like beef stew?"

Addie May's eyes lit up, overwhelmed by the idea of having a substantial meal for her siblings. They had been surviving on leftovers from the lodge for the past few weeks since their own food ran out. Tommy peeked out from behind the chair but wasn't ready to accept this stranger. Baby Girl danced around the floor with delight, although Sarah figured she was just a happy child and not responding to the arrival of a healthy meal. Addie May came over and peeked into the box and smiled when she looked up at Sarah. In addition to the items for the stew, there was milk, eggs, bacon, orange juice, peanut butter, and several loaves of bread.

"Thank you, ma'am," she said softly. "Papa will pay you back when he comes home."

Sarah pulled out the last few items as Addie May put the perishables in the small fridge. She placed packages of cake mix and brown sugar on the counter, along with a can each of pineapple and cherries. "Have you ever made a pineapple upside-down cake?" she asked Addie May with a mischievous look.

An hour or so later, young Tommy crept into the kitchen and held onto Addie May's arm as he whispered something to her. "Her name is Miss Sarah," Addie May responded and continued drying the utensils they had been using. The stew was simmering on one of the two burners that was still working, and Sarah was arranging the pineapple circles on top of the melted brown sugar and butter. She told Addie May to place a cherry in the center of each circle.

"I want one," Baby Girl demanded. Addie May looked at Sarah for permission.

"They're yours," was all she said and Addie May popped the cherry into the eager child's mouth.

"More! More!"

"That's all for now," Addie May responded firmly and Sarah noticed that the child accepted her sister's decision without argument.

"You're doing a good job with the children," Sarah said quietly while stirring the stew.

"Thank ya'," the girl responded with lowered eyes.

While the meal was cooking, Sarah sat down with the children and taught them to play I Spy. Ricky had come in earlier and didn't look surprised to see Sarah there. He just smiled and gave her an almost imperceptible nod. Baby Girl brought a tattered book from the bedroom and asked Sarah to read it. All the children crowded around, sitting at her feet and listened intently as if they hadn't heard the story many times before. When Baby Girl asked her to read it again, Sarah used funny voices for all the animals and was delighted to hear the children's laughter.

After dinner, Sarah and Addie May did the dishes and talked quietly. "Mary Beth said you would help find our Papa."

"I'll certainly try. My husband is coming to help us." She thought about what Mary Beth had told her and decided not to mention that Charles was a retired policeman. "He's very good at finding people," was all she said.

Addie May stopped drying the dishes and stood very still. She looked directly into Sarah's eyes and asked, "Do you think he's alive?" Sarah heard the girl's voice crack on the word *alive*.

"Addie May, we have to assume he's safe and that there's some good reason why he couldn't come back home. Let's just take it one day at a time."

"That's what I've been doing," the girl responded, reaching for the next dish to dry. "That and praying," she added. "So far, the Lord's taken care of us. We've had food on the table every day, … nothing like this, of course," she said with a grin and a sweeping motion referring to the delicious meal they had just enjoyed.

Coby had called Sarah's cell phone earlier in the afternoon to see when he should pick her up. Since things were going well, she told him to come whenever he was free before sunset. They were both surprised to find they had a cell phone signal and Sarah wondered about getting a phone for Addie May, although she probably didn't have anyone she could call other than Sarah. She decided to talk to Charles about it when he arrived.

When Coby came to pick her up, he said he was off for the day so he sat down with Sarah and the family and they devoured the cake and most of the milk. "I'll bring more tomorrow," she assured them, looking over at Coby with raised eyebrows.

"Done," he responded with a grin, knowing she had just asked him to pick up more milk.

Sarah and Coby were quiet on the ride back to the lodge. *If we can't find the father, that family won't be able to stay together*, she told herself feeling a lump in the pit of her stomach.

Chapter 16

By the time Sarah got back to the lodge, she barely had time to take a shower and get dressed before she heard the gentle knock at the door. Assuming it was Charles, she hurried to the door and was almost breathless when she opened it. But, to her surprise, Ricky was standing at the door, wearing shoes with broken laces and holding a small package wrapped in brown paper. "We want you to have this," he said shyly.

"What's this?" she said. "Come on in." She opened the door wide and the young boy reluctantly stepped over the threshold.

He looked around the room with big eyes and finally commented, "You rich?"

Sarah laughed and responded, "No, Ricky. Not at all. I don't live here; I'm just visiting. Now, what's this you brought me?"

"Addie May told me to bring you this. It was Mama's," he said, handing her the small package.

"Oh, Ricky, I can't take something of your mother's."

"Open it."

Reluctantly, she carefully removed the paper and found inside a gold locket embellished with a red stone in the shape of a heart. She gasped. "Oh! This is beautiful, and so delicate. But Ricky, I really can't take this. It should stay in your family."

"Addie May said it would bring you luck finding our dad." Sarah opened the locket and found a picture of a handsome young man. "Who's this inside? Your Dad?"

"Yeah, that's Papa."

"Your sister's right. This will help us find your father. We need a picture of him. So here's what I'll do." She glanced over and found him looking her in the eye eagerly, waiting for her response. "I'll remove the picture just for now and give it to my husband while he's searching for your dad. And I'll wear the locket for good luck. But when your father's home, we'll put the picture back inside and give the locket to Addie May to save for you children. How's that?"

Ricky blushed and looked at the floor for a moment, then raised his head and replied with a smile, "I like that." Sarah wanted more than anything at that moment to wrap her arms around this little boy and promise him everything would be all right, but she knew he wouldn't like to be hugged just yet, and she also knew that would be an empty promise. Instead, she extended her hand, and he shyly reached for it and they shook hands.

"It's a deal," she announced and smiled as she walked him to the door.

Moments later, there was another knock at the door, this time more forceful and determined.

As she opened the door, she and Charles fell into each other's arms "I don't ever want to be away from you that long again," her handsome husband said as he held her close to his heart.

* * * * *

"Where can we find a grocery store?" Sarah asked. She and Charles had finished breakfast at the lodge and were ready to head out to the Abernathy home. Turning away from the desk clerk and addressing Charles, she said, "I went through the cupboards and only found cornmeal and a few bags of beans. I think that's about all they've been eating."

"Turn left when you leave the lodge," the desk clerk responded. "Follow the dirt road down the mountain. It meanders a bit, but you'll hit the highway in about fifteen minutes. Turn right when you get there, and the market is just up the road on your left. It's nothing fancy.…"

"No problem. I just want to pick up a few things."

In fact, they left with five bags of groceries, much of the small shop's inventory.

All four children were happy to see her when Addie May opened the door, but they seemed reticent when they spotted Charles behind her. "This is my husband, Mr. Parker, and the man I told you about who's going to be looking for your father," she said as she sat two of the bags down on the sink. Charles carried the other three over and put them on the small kitchen table and spoke to the children.

Addie May came close to Sarah and whispered, "Miss Sarah, Papa wouldn't want us taking charity.…"

"I know, Addie May, but your father would want you children to have good food to eat. In the meantime, let's get some food in these children. Do they like bacon and eggs?"

Except for Tommy who had again taken up residence behind the chair, the children squealed with excitement.

Sarah and Addie May put the food away while Charles sat across from them in the living room. Sarah smiled to see Baby Girl crawl into his lap carrying the book. "Read me. Read me," she demanded.

"What's the baby's real name?" Sarah asked Addie May as she laid slices of bacon into the skillet.

"Papa was so upset when mama died, he couldn't tell them what to write down so they jist wrote Baby Girl Abernathy. I guess she needs a real name, but we've been calling her Baby Girl for so long, it seems like her name."

Sarah smiled and looked over at the little girl snuggled into Charles' arms with her thumb in her mouth and her ragged blanket held close. *I'll make her a little quilt when I get home*, she thought. Addie May saw a cloud pass over Sarah's eyes and asked if she was okay.

"Oh yes, I'm fine," she said knowing she had to keep her own doubts hidden from the children. *Where in the world is the father, and what will become of this family if he's never found?*

After breakfast, Sarah and Charles sat in the living room at Addie May's insistence while she and Ricky did the dishes. "Who's responsible for this nice fire?" Charles asked, looking at the blazing flames in the wood-burning stove.

"I did it," Ricky responded.

"Well, I helped," Addie May added.

"Me too, me too," Baby Girl called out, afraid she was going to be left out.

A playful argument ensued as each child, except Tommy, demanded his or her share of the credit. "Wait a minute," Charles interrupted. "It sounds to me like this was a family affair. You all did your part and it's a great fire." Then addressing just Addie May, he asked, "Is this your only source of heat?"

"We have a gas furnace but they cut the gas off last month. I guess Papa hadn't paid the bill. Anyway, we don't need it. This old stove of Grandpa's keeps us warm."

"Even in the bedrooms?" Sarah asked.

"We're all sleeping in Papa's bed while he's gone," Addie May responded. "We keep each other warm." Sarah knew she was keeping them more than just warm; she was helping them feel safe and loved.

Thinking about the bills for the first time, she asked Addie May, "How about the electricity bill. Do you …?"

"Mary Beth paid the bill last month. Papa will pay her back too," she quickly added.

Sarah and Addie May sat down at the kitchen table with a few sheets of paper from the notebook Charles always carried in his breast pocket. "It's habit," he had said.

Together they planned a few meals that Addie May could make. The young girl had never cooked a whole chicken and Sarah decided to cut it up so they could freeze portions. She checked the freezer compartment and, of course, found it empty. Most of the food she brought was canned since she thought that would be easiest for Addie May. Before she closed the refrigerator, she smiled seeing all the fresh fruit and vegetables.

"Okay, kids. Mr. Parker and I need to do some investigating. Is it okay if we look through your father's papers? We might be able to find out something about where he is."

"Him went to work," Baby Girl offered, speaking through her thumb.

Addie May tussled the little girl's curly hair as she led Sarah and Charles to her father's bedroom. Sarah felt a pang of sadness when she saw the four pillows neatly lined up across the head of the bed and the quilts folded at the bottom. Her heart went out to this vulnerable little family. "Papa keeps most of his papers in this drawer," Addie May said as she opened the top drawer of the dresser. "And there's a shoebox up there on that shelf, but I don't know what's in it."

Charles looked reluctant to handle her father's belongings and Addie May seemed to sense it. "Just spread it out on the bed or bring it into the kitchen table."

"Thank you, Addie May," Sarah said and gently slipped her arm around the girl's thin shoulder. Addie May leaned into Sarah ever so slightly and smiled up at her before turning and leaving the room.

Ricky shyly stuck his head in the room and said, "Can I help?"

"You sure can, Ricky," Charles responded. "Help me carry all this stuff into the kitchen table. There's more light out there." Together the three carried all the papers and the shoebox into the kitchen. Sarah and Charles sat down and began sorting through the papers. Ricky quickly became bored with the process and announced he was going outside. Tommy slipped on his jacket and followed his brother out the door.

Addie May sat down and held Baby Girl on her lap and sang very softly. Her voice reminded Sarah of the haunting tones produced by the young girl the night of the jamboree at the lodge. *That seems so long ago.*

Soon the baby fell asleep and Addie May carried her into the bedroom. Sarah peeked in later and saw that they were curled up together, both sleeping. She quietly spread a quilt over them. The baby sighed and snuggled closer to her sister.

"Let's put all these pay stubs together. They're from the mine here. That's the one that closed down, right? Isn't he working up in West Virginia?" Charles asked.

"That's what Mary Beth's father thinks, but he doesn't know where. Hopefully, we'll find a pay stub or something telling us where." They found bills, all with notations of the date they were paid, but nothing dated within the past six weeks. They found several unpaid electric bills, then one which settled all the previous ones with a carefully written notation that it was paid by Mary Beth the previous week. Charles put the unpaid gas bills in a pile and slipped them into his jacket pocket.

"How long has he been working in West Virginia?" Charles asked. "We should have found pay stubs."

"I don't know. Probably a few months. I know he was out of work for a long time."

"Maybe he kept them wherever he was staying during the week," Charles speculated.

"I wouldn't be surprised if he was living in his car."

"He could be bunking with somebody up there."

Later Sarah made sandwiches while Charles finished going through the papers and returned them to the dresser. Addie May rounded up the kids for lunch.

"Addie May," Charles began. "Can you think of any other place he might have been keeping papers, like maybe his pay stubs or other important papers?"

Addie May looked up as if a thought had just crossed her mind. "Once I found something in his pocket when I was washing his jeans. That one was ruined, but I reckon you could look in his other pockets."

"That's a great idea. Will you help me do that after lunch?"

"Sure," she said with a smile.

Later in the afternoon having had no success with the pocket search, Charles made a thorough search of the entire house and still there was no sign of a pay stub or any other evidence of where Mr. Abernathy was working. He did find a manila envelope tucked deep in one of the dresser drawers which contained Clara's death certificate and a birth certificate for Baby Girl Abernathy. There was also a letter from a local mining company announcing that they were closing the mine. *The guy's whole world fell apart that month*, he thought sadly.

Addie May, with Sarah's help, had a pot of soup simmering on the stove. "We'd better be going," he said, sounding discouraged. "I need to come up with a new strategy."

As they were saying goodbye to the kids, Charles spotted a flannel shirt hanging on a hook by the back door. "Is that your father's shirt?" he asked Addie May.

"Yeah, that's Papa's. I forgot about that one."

Charles walked over and took the shirt off the hook and immediately felt something in the breast pocket. Pulling it out, a smile spread across his face. "Mickelson Mining: Surface and Highwall Excavation, Bryston, Ohio," he read aloud.

Looking surprised, Sarah responded, "That's in northern Ohio. He couldn't possibly be working all the way up there, could he?"

"That's probably the main office, but they can tell me where he works. I'll get on the phone to them first thing in the morning."

The children were glowing with excitement, but Charles knew this business card offered no assurance their father would be returned to them.

Chapter 17

"Yes, we have a Richard Abernathy working at our Mickelson site in West Virginia. That's Operation 900B, located about twenty-five miles north of Beaver Creek. I can put you in touch with the foreman down there; I don't personally know Abernathy."

Charles took down the information and immediately dialed the number. "Could it really be this easy?" he said to Sarah as he put the call on speaker and waited for the foreman to answer.

Standing at the window of their room in the lodge, she responded, "I don't know, Charles. I don't have a good feeling about this."

"Stevenson," the voice bellowed into the phone. Charles explained who he was and that he was attempting to find Richard Abernathy. Stevenson didn't respond for a few moments, then repeated the name, "Abernathy, huh? I'd like to know what became of the man myself. I worked to get him assigned to an eight-days-on four-days-off shift so he could spend time with his family down in Tennessee and the next thing I know, he's gone."

"Gone?"

"Yeah. Just didn't show up one day. I was surprised; he'd seemed pleased about the assignment. I don't usually make concessions like this for new guys, but he was a good worker. Dependable. Well, at least until he stopped showing up," he added with a sarcastic snort. "He even left his stuff in his locker—just never came back. Do you want this stuff?" Stevenson added.

"Actually, I'd like to drive up and talk with you and maybe a few of the guys that knew him. I'd really like to track this guy down."

"You're a cop, you say? What did the guy do?"

"No, I'm retired from the force, and, as far as I know, the guy hasn't done anything. I'm just helping the family find him. He's got some kids down here who need him. How about I head up there tomorrow?" Stevenson gave Charles detailed directions from Beaver Creek to the site and said he'd pull a few guys together for him to talk to when he gets there.

"Ask for me at the gate, that's Marshall Stevenson."

Charles thanked the man and turned to Sarah. "Well, you heard. What do you think?"

"I don't know what to think. Nothing I've heard about the man indicates that he'd just take off and leave his family. I'm afraid something terrible has happened to him."

"I don't know, honey. People can do strange things under stress. You saw the things we found yesterday: a death certificate, a new baby without a mother, the mine closing. Just the financial pressures alone must have been overwhelming."

"Yes," Sarah agreed, "but he had a job. Granted, it was some 300 miles away, but he had something worked out. He had a plan. Why give up now?"

"We're not going to be able to answer that until we find the man and ask him, and I feel confident that we'll do just that."

Sarah shrugged. She definitely didn't share her husband's convictions.

"Do you want to ride up there with me tomorrow?" Charles asked. "It'll be a long day, but probably a pretty drive, mostly in the mountains."

"I'd like to spend the day with the children, if you don't mind making the trip alone. I want to teach Addie May how to make a few more easy meals and there's some mending to do. Besides, you don't know what you're going to find. You just might need to stay on a few days."

"Hmm, hadn't thought of that, but you may be right. Okay. I'll drop you off at their house when I leave in the morning, and you can call Coby when you're ready to come back to the lodge. I won't be back until very late; Beaver Creek is in southern West Virginia and will probably be at least a four-hour drive each way to the site. So what would you like to do today?"

"I'd love to show you Clingman's Dome and drive through the park. It's incredibly beautiful and the trees are starting to turn...."

"I'd like that," Charles responded, wrapping her in his arms. "I've hardly seen you since I got here. Let's take today just for the two of us."

* * * * *

The drive to West Virginia had, indeed, been spectacular. Charles hadn't spent much time in mountainous terrain and was tempted to stop at the various overlooks, but was eager to get this job done. The previous day spent with his wife had been relaxing. He had missed her more than he realized, but he was reminded how good it felt to be with the woman he loved. After so many years of being alone, he never expected to find love again, especially at this age.

Turning his attention back to the landscape, he noticed scars in the distance as if someone had taken a machete and sliced the top off the mountains. As he got closer, he saw trucks and bulldozers traveling up and down dirt roads that snaked their way up to the bare and flattened sites where men and equipment milled around like so many ants following their internal programs.

Reaching the gate to Mickelson Site 900B, he announced that he was there to see Marshall Stevenson. The guard, obviously expecting him, directed him to a construction trailer on the back side of the site. As he was driving away, Charles saw the guard place his cell phone to his ear.

Driving slowly along the gravel road which seemed to encircle the site, he saw a group of trailers parked along the edge, but one in particular stood out as a couple dozen men milled around it. He parked the rental car and walked toward the group which parted for him. A large, brawny man with a full beard and a baseball cap walked toward him. "You Parker?" the man called out above the grinding noise.

"Yeah. Stevenson?"

"You got it. Let's step inside. Billy?" he called to a disheveled looking man sitting at the desk, "Finish handing out these checks," he said, handing him a bundle of envelopes. Turning to Charles, he handed him one as well saying, "You might as well take this one." The name Richard Abernathy was scribbled across the front.

* * * * *

As Sarah was washing the dishes, Baby Girl announced, "Your purse is ringing."

Sarah hurried over, drying her hands on a tea towel she had purchased at a gift shop the previous day. "Hello?"

"Hi, Mrs. Parker. This is Mary Beth. I stopped by your room to see you, but you were gone. Are you with the children?"

"Yes, Charles brought me here early this morning. Addie May and I have been going over some recipes that her mother had in the cupboard. Has something happened?" she asked, surprised to be hearing from the young woman.

"No, but I remembered something this morning. When I was a little girl, Coby and I would visit the Jenkins and we'd play with Clara in the fields. What I remembered is that there was an older daughter. I never got to know her. She was always helping their mother with the chores; she was much older than Clara." Sarah slipped on her jacket as they talked and moved outside so the children wouldn't hear.

"That's interesting, Mary Beth. That means the children just might have family, although Addie May said she didn't know of any."

"Maybe she never met her. I remember hearing something about her living out west, but she was probably at the wedding when Richard and Clara got married. Dad might know more."

Sara could feel herself becoming hopeful. *This would mean the children might have someone to take care of them if the father's never found*, she thought reluctantly, not wanting to admit even to herself that it was a real possibility. "It would be wonderful if we could find family for them," she said. "Do you remember her name?"

"Rose? Rosie? Maybe Rosalie ... I just can't remember. Her last name would have been Jenkins at that time, but she's probably married now."

"I'll see what I can find out. I saw a few letters in the dresser when Charles and I were looking for pay stubs, but I didn't take the time to read any of them." Suddenly making the connection and getting excited, she added, "One was postmarked Oregon. Maybe it's from Clara's sister. The children just might have an aunt."

After they hung up, she asked Addie May if it would be okay to look at the letters. She explained that she thought there might be a relative they don't know about. "Aunt Rosie?" Addie May responded.

"You know your Aunt Rosie?" Sarah asked both surprised and just a little irritated that Addie May had assured her there was no family.

"No, I don't know her. I just know Mama had a sister, but we never saw her. There was some sort of problem, but I never knew what it was. She never came here and we never talked about her. I'm sorry I didn't tell you about her," Addie May added contritely. "I just don't think of her as family."

"It's okay," Sarah said, putting her arms around the girl. "I can see why you didn't think of her. Let's go get the letter."

* * * * *

Later that day, traveling down the mountain toward a peaceful green valley, Charles pulled over to the side of the road and dialed Sarah's cell phone. There was no response and he assumed she wasn't getting cell service again. He tried the room, and she answered on the first ring. "You're back already? How are the children?" he asked.

"They're fine. I called Coby around 2:00 to see when he could pick me up. He said he had a busy day and could come right over, or it would have to be after 8:00 in the evening, so I decided to come on back early. The kids were outside playing and Addie May wanted to start reading the book I brought her." She thought about telling him about the letter, but decided to wait until he got back to the lodge. "How did your meeting go at Mickelson?"

He told her what he had learned in talking with Stevenson and a couple of the men who worked with him. "He was headed home. They said he was eager to get home and had left directly from the worksite, not even checking out or picking up his things. I have his wallet."

"His wallet? Where was it?"

"It was in his locker under some work shirts. He must have forgotten it, but this gives me a more recent picture of him."

"He didn't have his license?"

"No."

"Did anyone know why he left so fast?"

"Nope. No idea. One of the men he worked with said he was excited about the new work schedule and maybe he was just eager to get home and tell his family. The new schedule has him home for four days between work shifts. No one had any idea why he never came back."

"Were they telling you everything?" Sarah asked, sounding as if she had questions.

"Well, I thought so until you asked that question. What are you thinking?"

"That maybe something happened there that they don't want to talk about."

Charles sat in the car without speaking. The idea slipped wordlessly into that part of his mind that usually picked up on subtle clues. *What's happening to me?* He knew that when he'd been on the job, this would never have escaped his attention. "You may be on to something," he finally said. "I need to go somewhere and think about this."

"Are you coming back to the lodge?" Sarah asked.

"I think I'll check into a motel in Beaver Creek and make some notes. I'm going back up there tomorrow," he added in a more determined tone.

Chapter 18

Sarah, showered and wearing one of her favorite flannel gowns, turned the covers down and propped the pillows up so she could sit up in bed. She reached for the book she had been reading, but changed her mind and picked up Rosalie's letter instead.

My dearest sister, she read.

> *I know you don't want to hear from me, but I must make one final attempt to reconcile. Beyond this letter, I won't bother you again. I want you to know that I love you and would never have purposely hurt you. Yet, I know I did cause you pain. If I had it to do over, things would have turned out differently. I wish you a lifetime of happiness, and I'll pray you see fit to forgive me someday.*

> *Your loving sister,*
> *Rosalie*

Rosalie, she thought. *This must be the Aunt Rosie that Addie May remembers hearing about.* No matter how many times Sarah read the letter, she found no hint of what had come between the sisters. The envelope was dated

1998 which meant it was written before the children were born and several years after Clara's and Rosalie's parents had died.

Since Addie May had never met her aunt, Sarah assumed she was holding in her hand their last contact. She wondered if Rosalie knew her sister had died. *Undoubtedly Richard let her know*, she thought. *But then …*

She slipped the letter back into the envelope.

* * * * *

"Good morning, love. I was hoping to catch you before you left. You're going to see the children today, aren't you?"

"I don't think so, Charles. It's raining and we made a huge casserole yesterday. I think I'll give the children a day to themselves."

"What will you do?"

"I'd like to do some sewing. A new quilting retreat started yesterday and I talked to the instructor about using one of their machines. She offered to have a portable brought up to my room. I thought I'd do something with the fabric I had left over from my project."

Sarah was still debating whether to tell him about the letter from the children's aunt, and she didn't know why she was hesitant. "What are your plans for the day?" she asked.

"I'm heading back up the mountain to Mickelson's. I spent the night in a motel on the outskirts of Beaver Creek and I started writing everything we know about Richard and his possible whereabouts. It only took three lines. I spent most of my time thinking about why the foreman would lie about how Abernathy left. If the foreman's lying, they must be covering up something, and all I can come up with is that maybe Abernathy was in some sort of accident on the site, and they're covering it up to avoid an investigation."

"Or maybe he learned something they didn't want him to know," Sarah suggested.

Again, Sarah had beat him to the draw. "I hadn't thought of that," he responded, somewhat dumbfounded. *What's happening to my investigative powers?*

Sarah wasn't surprised when he said that. She had noticed some subtle changes in him lately. She hoped it was just because their routine had been disrupted, but she vowed to get him to his doctor as soon as they returned home.

And that's the reason I'm hesitant to burden him with the letter, she told herself, suddenly understanding her unconscious motivation. *I'll handle this one myself.*

After they hung up, Sarah dressed and went downstairs for breakfast. Another quilt retreat was just beginning and the room was filled with excited quilters. She felt right at home. After breakfast, she went into the lounge where there was a coffee machine, several vending machines with sodas and snacks, and two computers, both on and ready to use.

She pulled the envelope out of her pocket and opened a search engine. She typed in Rosalie Burns, Portland, Oregon and a record popped up for a Jackson Burns with a forty-four year old associate named Rosalie. She clicked for more details and there was the address from the envelope. And now she had the phone number.

Fascinated with how quickly she was able to find Rosalie, she decided to try her own name. Not only did the search engine go directly to her record and announce her age for the whole world to see, but it presented a map of Cunningham

Village and an arrow on her house. "There's no such thing as privacy anymore," she grumbled as she stood up from the computer.

Back in her room, she pulled out her few scraps of material. She had over a yard left from her border fabric, but only bits and pieces of everything else. Suddenly she had a thought. She hurried downstairs to the manager's office to speak with Mary Beth's father, Jack Slocum.

"Mrs. Parker, glad to see you. I've been wondering if your husband's had any luck finding Abernathy."

Sarah caught him up on what they had each been doing and was sorry to tell him they had made no progress in finding Richard. "We do know where he was working," she added.

"Where?" he asked with interest.

"Up near Beaver Creek, West Virginia. It's a strip-mining outfit. ..."

"Not Mickelson's, I hope."

"You've heard of them?"

"Everyone around here has. It's a shady operation. I'm glad your husband has police connections. He just might need them.

For the first time, Sarah became worried for Charles' safety. She and Slocum talked briefly about what he had read in the papers and his own suspicions. "They tried to open an operation around here some twenty years ago, but we threw them out. A real shady outfit."

Sarah felt a knot twisting her stomach as she thought about Charles heading back to the work site.

"So, what can I do for you today?"

For a moment, Sarah forgot why she had come down to his office. The thought of Charles possibly being in danger had pushed her project to the back of her mind. "Oh," she finally said. "I was wondering if there's any way to get one more picture printed on fabric. I'm thinking about …"

Slocum interrupted her abruptly saying, "Absolutely. The class we have going on right now is working on that same project. If you give me your picture, I'll slip it in with the others that we're transferring to fabric."

"Wonderful," Sarah responded but without the enthusiasm she had when she first came up with the idea. "I'll run up and get the photograph now."

Once the picture was in Slocum's hand, she hurried back upstairs and dialed Charles' cell phone. It went immediately to voice mail.

Chapter 19

"Mrs. Burns, my name is Sarah Parker. I'm visiting here in Tennessee and have met the Abernathy children. I'm wondering if ..."

"Clara's children?" she asked. Sarah's heart sunk, fearing that Rosalie didn't know of her sister's death.

There was a deep sigh on the other end of the line. "I keep wondering what to do," the woman said. "I know Clara is gone; I learned about it from an old friend out there, but ..." She hesitated and then asked, "Who are you again?"

Sarah explained who she was and her relationship to the children. She told her about Richard's disappearance and heard the woman catch her breath. "Those poor children. Who's taking care of them?"

Sarah told her about Addie May and how she'd been functioning as the mother and homemaker since she was twelve. "That poor child," Rosalie repeated, over and over. "How are the other two? They're boys, right?"

"There are two boys, and then there's the baby," Sarah said.

"The baby? What baby?" Rosalie sounded confused at the mention of a fourth child.

"She's not exactly a baby. She's between two and three, I think. She's adorable. ..."

"How could there be a baby? Didn't Clara die over two years ago?"

"You don't know, do you? Clara died in childbirth. The baby lived."

"Oh my," the sister sobbed. "What a tremendous burden for little Addie May. Those poor children. What can I do?" Before waiting for an answer, she added, "I'll come get them and bring them here."

Sarah hoped she hadn't poked a hornet's nest by calling.

"I don't think they would want to leave their home right now," Sarah said as carefully as possible. "We're all hoping Richard will be found soon and back home with his children."

"He won't be back," she announced in an angry tone. "He's no good, and I tried to tell my sister that before she married him. Now he's run off and left those children. I was right about him, but Clara wouldn't listen." Changing the subject abruptly, she said, "How am I ever going to fit four children into this house ...?"

"Wait, please, Mrs. Burns ..."

"It's Rosalie. And your name again?"

I'm Sarah. Sarah Parker. I wanted to explain to you that my husband is a policeman." She didn't add that he was retired, "And he's looking for Richard. We are afraid something has happened to him and my husband, Charles, is following leads right now. I know the children wouldn't want to leave until they find out something about their father."

Rosalie was quiet. "Well," she said reluctantly. "Maybe I could wait until we know more if you're sure they're okay."

"I'm keeping a close eye on them, and I'll be able to stay on here for a few weeks. How about we just stay in close contact, and I'll keep you informed about what's happening. I can't tell you how happy I am to find that there's family. These children are so afraid of being separated and put into the foster care system."

"That will never happen," Rosalie assured her. "If they need a home, they'll have one here in Portland. I owe it to my sister."

* * * * *

"Sophie, your timing couldn't have been better! I'm so glad to hear your voice."

"I've been trying to call your cell, but nothing goes through."

"Reception up here is terrible. Since we're staying on, we're just using the hotel phone."

"So," Sophie began. "What's this about my perfect timing?"

Sarah began talking and hardly stopped to take a breath. She told Sophie about the children, about the shady operation and her fears for Charles, about the sister, and …

"Hold on, kiddo," Sophie interrupted. "You're overwhelming me. Let's go back to the shady operation. Tell me all about that and how it involves Charles."

Sarah slowed down and explained why Charles was in Beaver Creek and what had happened so far. She also told her about Slocum's suspicions and her own concerns for Charles. "He's on his way back to the worksite now to confront them. I'm so worried."

"He's a big boy, Sarah. He can handle folks like that."

Sarah didn't find much solace in Sophie's words. "I'm just worried about him, Sophie. He hasn't been quite himself since he got here."

"Tell me about the kids," Sophie said, changing the subject to something she thought would be more pleasant for Sarah. As it turned out, she was right. Sarah became very animated as she talked about the children, especially Addie May.

"The little one is called Baby Girl and is just adorable, but because she's the youngest, the other kids treat her like a baby doll. I don't know if they'll ever let her grow up," she said laughing.

"What about school?"

"Well, that's an issue no one is addressing just yet. They haven't been to school since the father disappeared and didn't go regularly even before that. ..."

"Aren't the authorities concerned?"

"I'm not sure there are authorities up here in the mountains. I do know that Addie May is worried about them getting separated and sent to foster homes, so she is probably playing it safe. She's taught the boys to read though and some simple math. She hasn't been to school herself since her mother died, what with the new baby and the chores."

"Whew. You really got yourself into a muddle up there, didn't you?"

"It's not all bad, Sophie. I've come to love these kids and, with any luck, this is going to work out. At least I've found a relative in Oregon, an aunt, who will take them if all else fails."

"I'm glad to hear that. I've been picturing you coming home with four children to add to your menagerie. By the way, how are those creatures of yours getting along?"

"Charles has been keeping up with the home front. Andy and Caitlyn are taking care of them. Barney is staying at Andy's house, but Boots chose to hold down the fort at home. By the way, could you walk up to Andy's and see how Barney is doing? I know he wonders what's happened to us."

"I'll do it, but I won't be able to help him. I don't speak dog. And speaking of dogs, you do know that Higginbottom's new SUV is still sitting in front of my house?"

"Oh my, I forgot all about that. Charles and I drove you to the airport, didn't we? Are you using it?"

"I don't have a key. I'm not sure what'll happen with it. I'm tempted to have it towed away, but something keeps me from doing that."

"Are you hoping he'll come back?" Sarah asked.

"Good grief, no!" Sophie bellowed. "I don't want to ever see that man again. What an loser he turned out to be."

"Are you okay?" Sarah asked gently.

"Yeah," she said softly. "Yeah, I'm fine. I was trying to make a silk purse out of the proverbial sow's ear. That man was one sow's ear for sure!" she added with a chuckle. "But it was fun dreaming. ..."

Sarah had enjoyed seeing Sophie in her playful, flirtation mode and hoped she wouldn't give up on the idea of having a man in her life. She clearly enjoyed the attention and being part of a couple.

"So, when are you coming home?" Sophie asked, interrupting her thoughts.

"Soon. I hope soon."

Chapter 20

Charles had spent the morning at Mickelson 900B and was on his way back down the steep mountain road. He realized he was no closer to finding Richard Abernathy than he was when he arrived. He knew where the man had been working; he knew when he supposedly left the work site. But where did he go? Assuming, of course, he ever left. His meeting with Stevenson and the project manager went nowhere, but he had to admit that he was inclined to believe them. "He simply drove away," Stevenson had said. "How would I know where he was headed?"

Charles drove directly to Beaver Creek sheriff's office, introduced himself, and asked to see the deputy in charge. A few minutes later, a pudgy man in rumpled work clothes emerged from a back room and greeted Charles.

"What can we do for you, detective?" he said extending a grease-stained hand but didn't offer his name. Noticing that Charles looked perplexed, he added, "Sorry about the attire. It's my day off, but I'm in here trying to deal with a plumbing problem. You know anything about toilets?"

"Not much," Charles responded, hoping to avoid having their meeting in the bathroom. "I'm looking for someone, and I was hoping you could answer a few questions for me."

"Doing skip traces are you?"

"Not exactly. I'm looking for a man who left his worksite up at Mickelson's and never arrived home. ..."

The man frowned. "Mickelson's, huh? Have you talked to them?"

Wanting to stay on this man's good side, he refrained from pointing out that going to Mickelson had been an obvious first step. "Yes," he said, "but they don't know what happened once he left there. I was wondering if you could take a look at this picture and tell me if you've seen him around."

"This is a driver's license," the nameless man responded. "The guy's driving around without this?"

"Presumably. Have you seen him?"

The man continued to look at the picture with interest. "Well ..." he responded without continuing. "It looks ... hey, Marvin," he called to the only other officer in the room. "Take a look at this. Does this guy look like that sketch we got from up in Bellmore?"

Deputy Marvin stood up from his desk and sauntered over. He stared at the picture for a few moments and finally spoke. "Yeah, he looks sort of like the guy. ..."

"Find me the sketch. It's not on the board."

"Sure, boss."

"And stop calling me boss. You aren't working in the bottling plant anymore. Call me sheriff, or sir, or even Cooper, but not boss."

When Marvin returned with the sketch, the three men hunched down over the desk and compared it to the picture on the license. "Could be the guy ..." mumbled the man who Charles now assumed was the sheriff.

"Yeah," Marvin added.

Charles remained quiet for a moment, then asked, "What's he wanted for?"

Marvin went back to his desk and brought the file. "Looks like low level stuff. Robbery of convenience stores up around Bellmore. It don't make a lot of sense, though, if he was headed for Tennessee. Bellmore's a few miles north of here."

"Who says he was headed home," the sheriff said.

Charles continued to look at the picture. *Why would Abernathy drive north and hold up a couple of convenience stores before heading home? This doesn't make sense.*

"Hold on," Marvin said frowning as he tried to remember the details. "I had a call from Marshton, across the line in Ohio. They're looking for someone with Tennessee tags who held up a small market in town. Could be the same guy."

"Why are they calling us?" the sheriff responded gruffly.

"They were calling around in a fifty-mile radius. They want the guy. There was a scuffle and the owner got hurt. He's also mayor of the town. He wants the guy punished."

"Well, we don't have him," the sheriff grumbled. "Don't know why people are always coming to us to solve their ..." His voice trailed off as he walked out of the room.

"Thank you, Sheriff Cooper," Charles called after him.

"Miles," the man hollered from what was apparently the bathroom. "Sheriff Miles. Sheriff Cooper Miles. No one ever gets it right," he grumbled as the toilet flushed. "Damn thing flooded again."

Charles turned to leave but stopped and spoke to the deputy. "How do I get to this Marshton? I'd like to run this picture past the mayor."

The officer gave him directions and, at Charles' request, called ahead to arrange for him to meet the mayor. "He'll be at the market this afternoon. You can get there is about forty-five minutes."

"Thanks," Charles said as he left.

An hour later Charles found himself on the outskirts of a small mountain town. The houses appeared to be built in the 1800s and opened right onto the street, which was probably wider now than when it was a dirt wagon trail. At the first corner, he spotted Brown's Market & Feed Store. He pulled around the corner, parked, and stretched as he got out of the car. *I'm getting too old for this*, he grunted as he flexed his arms.

"You that city detective?" the man said as Charles entered. "I'm Brown. That's Mayor Brown," he added, obviously proud of his position in the small town.

"Glad to meet you, Mayor. I'm Charles Parker; call me Charles. And I'm no city detective. I've been retired for some time now."

"So why are you working this case?"

"I'm not actually working the case, mayor. I'm helping a friend find a missing family member. The guy was working up north of Beaver Creek and he's gone missing. I just wanted to show you his picture and rule out the possibility that he's gotten into some illegal activities."

"Illegal activities? Walking in here and demanding my money is more than illegal activities. He'll rot in jail for this!" Mayor Brown's face became flushed and his voice became louder as he ranted. "He could've knocked me down when he pushed past me that way, you know?"

Charles pulled out the picture and laid it on the counter. "This the man?" he asked.

"Yeah. That's him," he responded frowning. "That's the man." He picked up the license and adjusted his glasses. "At least it could be … sure looks like him. Brown straggly hair and weak eyes."

"Weak eyes?"

"Yeah, you know … green. I never trusted a man with green eyes."

Charles' mind flashed to Baby Girl's big emerald green eyes. *What has happened to this guy? Why would he do this?* Charles shook his head and thanked the man. As he left, he wondered what he should tell Sarah. He knew he needed to pursue this, but it was going to break Sarah's heart.

He drove back to Beaver Creek and signed back into his motel room saying he'd probably stay a few days. "Where can a guy get a decent meal?" he asked the clerk.

She directed him up the street to an all-night café. "Cops eat there all the time," she added. *Do I still look like a cop?* he wondered as he headed toward the room.

He knew he had to call Sarah, but decided to put it off until after he ate. He was feeling a little woozy, and his eyes weren't focusing too well. *I need sleep*, he told himself. He laid across the bed and slept until his cell phone rang in the middle of the night. He put the phone to his ear, but didn't say anything.

"Charles?"

"Who's this?" he mumbled. "Sarah?"

"Of course, it's Sarah. What happened to you? I've been so worried."

"I'm ..." He looked around the room trying to connect with his environment. *Where am I?* Things slowly came into focus and he realized he was in the motel room. "I'm so sorry, hon. I just laid down for a minute, but I guess I fell asleep. What time is it?" His curtain was still open; it was dark out, but the lights from the parking lot flooded his room.

"It's 2:30 in the morning, Charles. I've been beside myself with worry. The last time I heard from you, you were getting ready to go into Mickelson's. I had no idea what happened to you after that, but my imagination has been going crazy."

"I'm so sorry, hon. I have no excuse. I really don't know what happened. I was going to call after I ate...." Thinking back, he added, "I guess I never ate either."

"I'm worried about you, Charles. Are you feeling okay?"

"Sure, honey. I'm just a little tired. Maybe I should come on back, but I might be on to something. Maybe I should stay up here. I don't know...." He realized he was having trouble thinking straight. "I'm not sure...."

"Charles, go back to sleep. Get a good night's sleep. Get some breakfast in the morning and then call me. You'll feel better in the morning, I'm sure." But she wasn't so sure. She'd never heard him expressing confusion or being hesitant to make a decision. "Call me after breakfast, okay?"

"Okay." He hung the phone up and turned over on his side to get away from the blinding lights in the parking lot. He wondered if he had said goodbye. He wondered if he should. ... He drifted back into a very deep sleep.

Chapter 21

"Good morning, my love. Have you forgiven me?" He sounded rested and chipper.

"Of course, Charles. I wasn't angry; I was just scared. I didn't know what had happened to you, and I played back all the stuff Slocum told me. I was afraid of what might have happened to you at the mine."

Charles chuckled, but immediately apologized. "Sorry, dear. I didn't mean to laugh, but you make this sound so cloak and dagger. I interviewed the guys again, and I believe them, more or less."

"More or less?"

"Okay. I could be wrong, but they sound like they're on the up and up."

"You said you have some other leads?"

"Nothing really concrete. Just a few things I'm checking out. I'll fill you in when I get a little farther along."

Sarah remained quiet. *There's something he doesn't want to tell me.* She decided to trust his judgment and not push. But for the children's sake, she hoped it wasn't bad news. "Okay," she said finally. "Please tell me when you know more. It's hard being here and not knowing what's happening. I wish I had gone with you. ..."

"The children need you there." Changing the subject, he added, "What have you and the kids been doing?"

"Addie May and I are having a great time," she responded with renewed enthusiasm. "She pulled her mother's sewing machine out of the attic, and I brought a few pieces of fabric and thread. We started a little quilt for Baby Girl."

"Baby Girl," Charles repeated. "I wish she had a real name."

"The children and I talked about that. They had a wonderful idea that we'll present to their father when he comes home."

"Are you allowed to tell me?"

"I think I can. They want to name her Clara for her mother. They all agreed."

"Even Tommy?"

"Especially Tommy!" she responded. "He's spending more time with me now and is actually talking once in a while. Just yesterday, he said, 'I like soup,'" Sarah announced with a glimmer in her voice, which he knew from experience corresponded to a glimmer in her eyes. "So what are your plans for today?" she asked.

"I'm thinking about hanging around here for a day or two. I want to talk to a few people, maybe find out where he'd been staying. You never know where the leads will come from." He felt bad about stretching the truth, but he didn't want to mention the possibility that Abernathy may have gotten himself into trouble. He hoped that talking to some of the shopkeepers could put him on the man's trail. "Somewhere there's someone who knows something, and

I'm going to try to find that person. I'm heading over to the sheriff's office now."

"You have reason to believe the sheriff will know something?" she asked, now suspicious.

Oops. I said too much. I forget how astute this woman is. "Of course," he said jokingly. "We cops know everything!"

He drove across town to the Beaver Creek sheriff's office and asked for Sheriff Miles. "Not in today," Marvin announced. "It's hunting season. He'll be back in a couple of days. Anything I can do for you?"

"I've been wondering if you have any reports about other holdups."

"Just in our jurisdiction. We don't communicate much state to state on these little things. Missing children, now, that's another story. And kidnappings. Do you suppose your guy was kidnapped?"

"No, I doubt that. Could you tell me where some of the holdups occurred in your jurisdiction?"

"Sure." Marvin pulled out a stack of papers from his inbox and walked over to the wall map. "Grab them pushpins over there," he said to Charles. Scanning through the papers he said, "Okay, there was one here, just to the east of us, and another over here near the state line."

"That's Virginia over there?"

"No, that's Kentucky. On down here, that's Virginia. We've got four states meeting within fifty miles of us … lots of jurisdictions to deal with and since he hit Ohio, I'm thinking he's probably traveling around."

"Do you folks share information?"

"Yes, on the big stuff, but these are triflin' things—a few dollars here and there, ma and pa places, no one hurt.

We just hope we catch them in the act, but we don't go searching that much. We definitely don't fax reports across jurisdictions for this kind of stuff," he admitted.

"I'd like to find out if it's my guy," Charles said.

"So I suggest you check out these two places in our jurisdiction first. It seems like he struck around here for a while. Might still be here."

Charles took the addresses, fed them into his GPS, and headed for the first town on Marvin's list. It was another mountain town but this time more urban than Mayor Brown's town. He pulled up in front of the sheriff's office and saw they had meter parking. He pulled a few quarters out of his pocket, deposited them, and headed inside. He asked to see the deputy in charge of the string of robberies that had occurred recently. A young man with a crew cut, wearing a crisp uniform and freshly polished shoes, appeared and led him to an inner office.

"I don't know if I'd call it a string," the deputy said as he brought out a few files for Charles to look at. Pulling out the various witness descriptions and looking at the picture Charles had, the deputy remarked, "Could be your guy. The description fits. The car … well, one guy said it was blue, another saw black, but that happens. Several witnesses saw Tennessee tags but no one saw the number. That happens too, but I don't know how. You either see it or you don't, ya know what I mean?"

Charles nodded his head in agreement, carefully reading the details of the robberies. "He never got much, a few dollars here and there. Just enough, I guess, to keep going."

"Yeah," the officer agreed. "Gas money and a meal here and there. He's probably living in his car. I imagine the guy's starting to feel a little desperate, not desperate enough to hurt anyone though."

"Well, there's a guy over in Ohio claims to have been injured, but it's doubtful."

"Nah. This guy isn't dangerous. Just getting along best he can. But the shopkeepers want it solved."

"I'd like to talk to these shopkeepers if that's okay."

"Sure. Help yourself. Just let me know if you learn anything new."

"Agreed.

"By the way," the officer said as Charles was leaving. "You say he'd been working up near Beaver Creek?"

"Yeah. Strip mine."

"Not Mickelson's, I hope."

Charles stopped in his tracks. "Yes, Mickelson's. Why?"

"They're bad news. Had a couple of disappearances up there a year or two ago. Never solved as far as I know. It was before my time."

Charles gave a deep sigh as he slumped into the driver's seat of his rental car. "Damn," he mouthed under his breath. "Now what?"

After thinking it over, Charles headed for a fast-food restaurant with only two cars outside. He figured he could get coffee and some privacy. He chose a booth toward the back and dialed his son in Denver.

"John, it's Dad." They chatted awhile, but Charles quickly got to the point. "I won't go into all the details now, but I'm tracking a man who's gone off the radar up in West Virginia. ..."

"You're in West Virginia?" John exclaimed.

"I'll get to that. Anyway, this guy was working for a strip-mining outfit that I've heard some bad stuff about. For one, there are rumors about some unresolved disappearances at the mine. I'm wondering if your FBI friend might be able to find out what's going on up there. I'm afraid my guy might have gotten caught up in something bad."

"That's my friend Seymour. I can call him and see if there's an investigation going on. But Dad, this sounds like dangerous business. I hope you're staying clear of the mine. Let the professionals deal with it."

Charles was quiet for a moment. It was hard to hear that he was no longer one of those professional that people let deal with it.

"Sorry, Dad. You know what I mean. You don't have an entire department behind you now. You can't put yourself out there alone."

"That's true," Charles conceded. They talked a while as Charles sipped his coffee. He agreed to continue his own investigator of the local robberies and wait to hear what Seymour might be able to find out about Mickelson's. He could only hope Abernathy wasn't involved in anything at the mine. *He'd be better off being the small-time crook!*

As he was driving toward the next town on his list, he felt a sudden urge to keep going. He had just passed a road sign indicating he was pointed toward Fort Stewart, Kentucky. He pulled over and checked his map. It looked like a likely town if Abernathy was actually making the rounds. He queried his GPS about police stations in Fort Stewart and two came up. "Bigger town that I realized," he said aloud.

He chose the one closest to the highway and continued up the road.

The highway was essentially empty, so Charles set the cruise control. He needed time to put the pieces together. *If Sarah were here*, he thought, *I'd simply lay the facts out and she would listen, and somehow it would all come together.* He thought about pulling over and calling her, but he still wasn't ready to tell her about the robberies.

In an attempt to gain some perspective, Charles decided to go through what he knew so far. *First of all*, he told himself, *the consensus seems to be that Abernathy is Beaver Creek's small-time crook.* Turning that thought over in his mind, he added, *but it just doesn't sit right with me. Everything I know about the man says this just isn't his style.* "On the other hand," he said aloud, looking around to make sure he wasn't being observed, "I never even met the man, so how can I say *what* he's capable of?"

Several trucks had joined him on the highway, so he turned off the cruise control. He continued to mull over the facts in his mind. *Sarah has total confidence in the man*, he told himself, *but the fact is she doesn't know him either!*

Charles realized there was sweat running down his forehead. He wiped it away with his shirt sleeve and decided to stop at the next opportunity. *And why am I driving from one robbery site to another asking if this is the man? They all say they think it's him. What am I doing? Am I trying to catch a crook or find a father? And if I do find him, will I turn him in? Sarah is expecting me to bring him back to his family.*

He was experiencing that odd feeling of confusion again and was having trouble focusing on the road. *Is something wrong with my glasses?* He slipped them off and looked at them, but they appeared to be fine. He again wiped the sweat from his eyes.

He spotted a sign for a fast-food restaurant at the next exit and moved over to the right-hand lane. A deep horn sounded behind him and he saw the driver struggling to maintain control of his truck. *I didn't see him at all.* Shaking, Charles pulled onto the shoulder to apologize, but the truck flew past him. *I can imagine the language that man is using right now and I don't blame him!*

Chapter 22

"So, here's my plan," Sarah began, sitting in the visitor's chair next to Jack Slocum's desk. "I want to help Addie May make a quilt to give to their father when he returns. The other kids can help, and it would be a really positive family project. They're getting a little doubtful about his return, and I think this would give them a boost."

"I like the idea, Sarah, but how can we help?"

"I need fabric, and I know the instructors have baskets of scraps, and I'm going to ask Brenda if they would donate a few pieces for the children's project. Also we need a back, and I'm hoping you can spare a sheet from the lodge's linen supply."

"Absolutely," Jack replied. "In fact, I have a few flannel sheets that the guests don't seem to like. Would one of those work for a back?"

"That would work perfectly, and perhaps we could have one more to use as batting."

"Not sure what batting is, but you're welcome to as many as you want. Let's walk over to the classroom and talk to Brenda about the fabric."

As they were leaving his office, Slocum stopped and looked at Sarah. "Sarah, you've got to be a very special person to set your own life aside and help this family. You don't know how much we all appreciate what you're doing."

"I've grown to love this little family, Jack. Charles and I really want to help them."

The class was in session with machines buzzing away. Slocum motioned for Brenda to come out into the hall. He told her about Sarah's project and Brenda was immediately excited about it. "I have baskets and baskets of scraps, Sarah. Come on in and take what you need." Sarah followed her into the classroom, and together they pulled several baskets out of the closet.

"What are you girls up to?" one of the students asked.

"Tell them what you're doing, Sarah."

Sarah, no longer shy about speaking in front of a group after all the classes she'd taught at her quilt shop, explained what she had in mind. They wanted to know what pattern she would use, and she said that she thought the children would understand a simple four-patch better than the more complicated blocks. "And it will be easy for the thirteen-year-old to sew."

"How will you quilt it?" someone asked.

Before Sarah could respond (she actually hadn't thought this far ahead), another student spoke up saying, "Why don't you tie it?" She reached into her enormous tote bag and pulled out a skein of yarn and handed it to Sarah. "You're welcome to this; I brought more than I need."

Sarah thanked the woman profusely, but had to admit she hadn't tied a quilt and wasn't sure how. "Let's have a quick lesson in tying," Brenda said. She directed the class to come up to the front of the room, and she quickly stacked two layers of fabric with a piece of batting in the middle. She then demonstrated how to pin the quilt and then how to make a secure square knot. "Leave some of the yarn dangling," she added. "It looks pretty."

"This will be a good job for the boys," Sarah commented as she watched.

As she was leaving the room, everyone wished her good luck with her project and one woman handed her a plastic bag filled with safety pins. "You'll be needing these," she said with a smile. Sarah was reminded what generous people quilters are.

Before she reached the elevator, Jack Slocum came out of his office carrying a manila envelope. "This is for you," he said handing her the envelope. "The photo came out really nice on the fabric." She thanked him and took it to her room.

Laying the fabric photograph next to her fabrics, Sarah realized she had chosen well. The photograph was of her two children, Martha and Jason, with her granddaughter, little Alaina, curled up in Jason's arms. Martha was wearing an aqua dress which perfectly matched the aqua in the turquoise and aqua fabric she intended to use as a border. "This will make a perfect wall hanging," she told herself, "but that project will have to wait." She quickly dialed Coby's cell phone and left him a message, "I'm ready whenever you are."

As she was hanging up, there was a knock at the door and a voice called, "Sarah, it's Mary Beth with your flannel sheets." She opened the door and invited her in. She excitedly told Mary Beth about the project she had planned for the children.

"What have you heard from your husband?" the young girl asked. "Is he having any luck?"

Sarah's face fell a bit as she began telling Mary Beth what little she knew about the search. "He seems to be onto something, but he's not very forthcoming about it. I think he doesn't want to upset me, but not knowing upsets me even more. I'm just hoping for some good news soon."

Sarah's phone rang and Mary Beth headed quickly toward the door. "Gotta get back to work," she said as Sarah answered the phone while nodding her thank you.

"I'm on my way back to the lodge," Coby reported. "I can take you over to the Abernathy's in about twenty minutes."

"Perfect. I'll wait on the porch."

* * * * *

Charles was entering the city of Fort Stewart, just over the border into Kentucky. It had been a long time since he'd experienced busy streets and urban sprawl. As he came into the downtown area, traffic became heavy and he was relieved to hear his GPS announce that the police station was immediately on his left. He spotted a car pulling away from the curb and quickly grabbed the parking place. *I don't think Abernathy would have spent any time here,* he told himself, *knowing this was certainly not what the mountain man was accustomed to.*

He went inside and told the desk sergeant what he was after. Frowning, the officer placed a call and an aging detective made his way partway up the hall, motioning for Charles to follow him to his office. "We hear about this kind of crime, but, you know, we can't do much about it. We've had two murders just this week over by the park. Our guys are working round the clock." He thumbed through some papers and added, "Nah. I don't have anything for you."

Charles thanked him and was heading for the door when the detective added, "But I heard about a bad situation just over the line in Virginia. It was a simple nickel-and-dime-type robbery gone bad. I heard there was a shooting."

"Where was that?"

"Down in Caraway, Virginia. It's about twenty miles below Beaver Creek heading south."

Charles remembered seeing the sign when he was driving up from Tennessee. "I'll check it out on my way back home," he said and he thanked the man for his time.

"Bradford's Bait & Tackle Shop," the detective called after him as Charles was heading down the hall. "Don't know how I remembered that ... just thought it was a strange place to think about robbing. What's the guy hope to get, worms?"

Charles was getting tired. *I don't know how I did this for all those years. I'm worn out.* He drove back to the motel in Beaver Creek and decided to go ahead and spend the night. "I'll be checking out early in the morning," he told the desk clerk as he settled up.

"Hi, sweetie," he said when Sarah answered the phone. It made him feel relaxed to hear her voice. He had showered and hoped to get a good night's sleep. He'd be glad to get back to their comfortable life in Middletown.

She told him about the quilt she was making with the children. "I've taught the boys how to make square knots and they can hardly wait for Addie May and me to finish the quilt. Baby Girl spent today choosing fabrics from the basket. Her daddy's quilt will have lots of owls, bears, and kittens," she said laughing.

"He'll love it." Charles realized his tone lacked enthusiasm; he was beginning to doubt that Richard Abernathy would ever be returning to his family. The disappearances at Mickelson had crept back into his mind, and he wondered if Abernathy had simply become one more man who vanished from the site. He contemplated all the possible places a body could be hidden at a mining operation.

"Where have you gone?" Sarah asked, aware that he had drifted off.

"Just detecting, sweetheart, in my mind."

"No luck finding him, I guess?"

"No. I'm coming on home tomorrow. I have one stop to make, but I should be home by midafternoon."

"Home. When did we both start thinking of Ten Oaks as home?" she asked rhetorically.

Chapter 23

A road sign indicated that Caraway was thirty-two miles from the exit.

Charles didn't realize Caraway was that far off his route. He pulled over at the exit to consider whether the detour was worth it. *Why do I need another person saying "yeah, that looks like the man" unless he can also tell me how to find the man?* But then he remembered the officer had said this one involved a shooting. *What if Abernathy's been sitting in jail all this time!*

Feeling suddenly hopeful, he started up the rental car and turned onto the exit ramp. Traveling to Caraway was slow. A two-lane road crawled up and down the mountains ultimately coming to a small town nestled in a secluded valley. *Abernathy would have been a fool to drive all this way to hold up a tackle shop*, he told himself.

"Caraway Population 386," the sign announced.

There were only a few stores on the main road through town—the post office, a market, a service station that appeared to be closed down, and Bradford's Bait & Tackle Shop on the corner. He parked and went in. The tingling of a small bell brought an elderly man in overalls out of the back room. "Kin I hep ya, young feller?"

Young fellow. Charles smiled. "It's been a while since I've been called a young fellow," he responded.

"Everyone's a young feller to me," the man said in a gravelly voice. "What kin I do fer ya?"

"I'm up from Gatlinburg looking for a man. I heard you had a robbery here, and I was hoping ..."

"You betcha I had a robb'ry. The guy didn't get nothing though."

"Can you tell me about it?"

"Well, sir, I'll tell ya. This guy comes in and says he has a gun, an' I should give him my money. Well, sir, I don't see no gun, and I told him so. He put his hand in his pocket. I told the police all this before."

"I know. I'd just like to hear what happened. So he reached for his gun?"

"Don't know. Put his hand in his pocket. My grandkids were playin' in the back room. I won't take no chances with them young'uns. I pulled my gun out from under the cash register and I shot him."

"Dead?" Charles asked with a sinking heart.

"Deader than an old rusty door nail. I told them cops all this. They said I didn't do nothin' wrong. I was protectin' my place and the young'uns." He was becoming defensive and Charles quickly spoke up to reassure him, hoping not to get shot himself.

"You were right. You were protecting your family. Do you know who this guy was?"

"Never heared his name. It was in this paper here." He pulled out a well-worn newspaper which had obviously been passed around among many customers. Charles read aloud, "Man killed during robbery attempt at Bradford's Bait & Tackle Shop in Caraway, Virginia." Charles quickly scanned through the details which were presented much like the old man had told it to him. Several paragraphs went into the fact that this was the first criminal fatality in the past twenty-five years, and two more paragraphs told about other crimes that occurred in the quiet town of Caraway over the past years. Charles searched for a name. Finally, toward the end of the article, he read, "The victim, Robert Mattington from Richmond, Virginia, was said to have an extensive police record for robbery, breaking and entering, and assault."

"I'd like to ask you a question, Mr. ...."

"Hessen," the man responded. "The name's Hessen."

"Okay, Mr. Hessen ..."

"Not *Mr.* Hessen. Just Hessen."

With a deep sigh, Charles continued. "Okay, Hessen. I'd like to show you a picture. Is this the man you shot?" He pulled out the driver's license he was now carrying in his shirt pocket.

"That's him," he said, looking at the picture. "Wait a dang minute," he said as he reached behind the counter and pulled out a large magnifying glass. He studied the picture again. "Nah. That ain't our guy. Looks like him, but ain't him. Different nose."

Charles went back to the car, not sure what to believe. *Richard Abernathy may well be dead*, he told himself sadly. He went back in and asked for the name of the police officer Hessen had dealt with. He then drove up the street a few blocks and parked in front of an abandoned trailer. He placed a call to the number on the card Hessen had given him.

"Michaels," the officer answered on the first ring. Charles explained who he was and why he was calling. He asked if the victim in the Bradford tackle shop shooting had been positively identified.

"Absolutely," Officer Michaels responded. "His sister came down and personally identified the guy. Long history with the police she told me. Fingerprints on file. It was a positive ID." Charles sighed with relief. *I may not know where he is, but at least Abernathy didn't die in a bait and tackle shop.*

"Any chance he'd been up around Beaver Creek."

"Good chance," Michaels responded. "Sister said he'd been visiting friends up in West Virginia." Charles gave him Sheriff Miles' number and suggested he give him a call. "You might be able to close a few cases for the guy."

"Happy to," Michaels responded. "Not much going on around here now that our only criminal in twenty-five years is dead."

Charles turned the car around and began the thirty-two-mile drive back to the highway. "So I've wasted several days tracking down the wrong man," he admonished himself. *I'll go back to the drawing board and ask the question I started out with: what happened to Richard Abernathy when he left his work site over six weeks ago, assuming he actually did leave the site alive.*

Over the past week, Charles reminded himself, he had talked to police stations and hospitals. He'd called the morgue in several jurisdictions just to be on the safe side. Nothing. He then followed a hunch which lead him through four states and ended at a bait and tackle shop in a town with a population just under four hundred.

When he reached the highway almost an hour later, he sat at the ramp contemplating his next step. *Do I go north and demand answers from Mickelson's or do I go south and back to Sarah?*

"Sarah wins, hands down," he announced and he headed south.

* * * * *

Sarah dialed Charles's cell phone again. She had left several messages and was getting worried. It was after 9:00 and he still hadn't arrived. "He said he'd be here in the midafternoon," she told Sophie, "and he's still not here."

"He's a big boy. He'll be along soon. You said he had a stop to make. It must have taken longer than he expected." To help Sarah get her mind off worrying, Sophie asked about the children again. "Tell me what you and the kids did today."

Sarah immediately brightened up. "I taught Addie May how to sew the squares into four-patches before I left yesterday. That child must have stayed up half the night. They were mostly done when I got there this morning. We laid them out on the bed and the kids arranged them the way they wanted them. Addie May was putting rows together when I left. She's quite a little quilter. I wish we had time to do more."

"Does that mean you're coming home soon?"

"I don't know, Sophie. Charles is sounding discouraged. At some point, we'll have to give this up and admit the man is gone."

"What about the children?"

"That would mean they'd be moving to Portland, I guess. I can't really picture these adorable mountain children living in the big city. I think they'd be overwhelmed by it all."

"Kids adjust," Sophie responded.

"That's not really the kind of adjustment I'd like to see them make. You should see these mountains. It's beautiful and serene. A wonderful place to live." Sarah became quiet.

"You aren't thinking about moving out there, are you?"

"Oh no, Sophie. Absolutely not. But I know the children would miss it."

"One thing to think about Sarah, they won't miss having to fend for themselves. They'll have a warm, safe home and they'll get an education."

"That's true. I just so hoped … Sophie, someone's trying to get through on this phone. Maybe it's Charles. I'll call you back."

Pushing the call-waiting button, she said, "Hello?"

"Mrs. Parker?"

"Yes?"

"This is Doctor Graham from Johnson City Memorial Hospital. We have your husband here and …"

"What?" Sarah responded, instantly in a state of shock. "What do you mean?"

"Mrs. Parker. Your husband had a stroke this afternoon. He was traveling near Johnson City and was brought to our hospital here." He could only hear gasps on the other end of the line. "Mrs. Parker, are you okay?"

"Is he …?" she wanted to ask if he was alive, but didn't want to hear the answer. *Has my own heart stopped beating?*

"Mrs. Parker, Your husband is going to be just fine," the doctor said, attempting to get her attention. She was obviously in shock and not understanding.

"Was there an accident? What happened?"

"Your husband had a stroke. It was a mild stroke and there's evidence that he may have experienced a few other incidents over the last few days but nothing serious, I assure you."

"Incidents?" she repeated. "What kind of incidents?"

"Transient ischemic attacks or TIAs. These are small strokes with no lasting damage. We see this pattern as a warning and your doctor will talk to you about medication and life style changes when you get home. For now, your husband is fine."

"He had a serious stroke a few years ago. …"

"I know. He told me, and I've talked with his doctor in Middletown. We've increased his medications, and I'd like to keep him here for a day or two just to watch his vitals. He's fighting me on that one. …"

"Tell him I said for him to stay and that I'm coming as soon as I can get there," she responded, sounding more coherent. "When can I talk to him?"

"You can call him in about a half hour. He's being admitted to a room right now. He'll be in room 228B." He gave her the phone number for the hospital.

"Where are you?" she asked.

"We're in Johnson City, about two hours from you." The doctor gave her the address of the hospital and waited patiently while she wrote it down.

"Mrs. Parker, Do you have someone to bring you? You shouldn't drive those winding roads at night."

"I'll get a ride," she responded.

Sarah thanked the doctor, sat down on the bed and wept. "I can't lose this man," she muttered. "I can *never* lose this man."

Chapter 24

Before calling Charles, she put a call in to the downstairs desk to see what sort of transportation the lodge might be able to arrange for her. She was reluctant to ask Coby to make a four-hour round trip during the night when he had to work the next day. It was already past 10:00.

The desk clerk put her on hold and a few moments later, Jack Slocum came to the phone. "Mrs. Parker, how can I help you?"

"I didn't mean for them to disturb you, Mr. Slocum. I was just asking if there might be some form of transportation available. My husband ..." Her voice cracked as she told him the story.

"I can send Coby ..." he started to say, but Sarah interrupted him.

"I don't want to pull Coby out this late. Maybe I should just wait until morning, but ..."

"Mrs. Parker, remember, Coby is more than an employee here; he's my son. Of course, I'll send him right over. You might even need him to come get you later tomorrow. Coby will be at your disposal until your husband is back with us. Now, what else can we do to help you right now?"

"I'm going to call Charles and tell him I'm on my way. Just send Coby over whenever he's ready. And Mr. Slocum, thank you."

"You are very welcome, Mrs. Parker. Whatever we can do."

Sarah splashed water on her face and freshened her makeup, as if Charles could see her when she called.

* * * * *

"Good morning, my love," Charles said softly as he looked at his bride sleeping in the chair.

Sarah opened her eyes and saw that Charles was awake and smiling at her from his bed. She had been sleeping in a recliner pulled close to him. When she arrived during the night, Charles had opened his eyes and smiled at her but had drifted right back into medicated slumber.

Standing, she realized that she was stiff in places she didn't know she had. *I guess I'm a bit too old to be sleeping in a chair*, she admonished herself. They had offered her a cot but she had refused, thinking she would stay awake and make sure Charles was okay. "I guess I fell asleep," she responded as she straightening her clothes and fluffing up her hair. "How are you feeling this morning?"

"Like a million dollars now that you're here. How about springing me and we go get sausage and pancakes."

"We'll talk to the doctor about having that meal some other time; right now your breakfast is arriving." She watched as the orderly raised the head of his bed and arranged the tray for him.

"Yum," Sarah said with pretend enthusiasm. "Oatmeal and dry toast."

Turning to the orderly, Charles said, "Well, my wife seems to like this meal. How about we give it to her, and you bring me sausage and pancakes."

Not sure how to react, the orderly responded. "Can't do that sir, but I can get her a tray like this one."

"Great idea. Would you do that please?" He smiled at Sarah in his usual mischievous way, and it brought tears to her eyes.

"I see you're back," she said kissing his forehead.

As they ate, the nurse came into the room and took his vitals. She asked him about a bed bath and he told her he was perfectly capable of taking a shower. Later Doctor Graham came in and formally introduced himself to Sarah. He was glad to see that she had overcome her initial response to her husband's illness and was now asking all the right questions about his care.

"Just see your doctor when you get home," he responded, turning to Charles. "He's expecting you."

"He will," Sarah spoke up in a take-charge tone. "He will."

Later that morning, after convincing Charles he would be staying one more night, Sarah asked him to tell her exactly what had happened.

"Darned if I know. The road just got fuzzy and I got very weak. I pulled over and I think I might have gone to sleep. I don't know for sure, but the next thing I knew some guy was helping me out of the car and into an ambulance. I kept telling them I was fine, but no one was listening. Then I was hooked up to all these monitors.... How did you find out?"

oven, Sarah thought about Charles and his vegetable plate at lunch. *I'll make sure they give him a hearty meal tonight*, she told herself.

"Miss Sarah," Addie May began as they were doing the dishes, "did Mr. Parker find our papa?"

"No, Addie May. He didn't." She couldn't lie to this girl and continue to give her false hope, but she wasn't ready to tell these children that it was conceivable that their father might never return. "Mr. Parker and I haven't had a chance to talk about the next steps, but we'll make sure you kids are cared for no matter what."

"You don't think he'll be back, do you?" she said softly, with her eyes lowered.

"I'm not ready to say that, dear. Mr. Parker and I are going to be talking about this tomorrow when he's feeling better, and we'll see if there's anything else we can think of to do. I just don't want you worrying. Like I told you the other day, your Aunt Rosie loves you and will make sure you have a home. You'll never be alone with all this responsibility again."

It broke Sarah's heart to see the one tear slowly run down the girl's cheek. As quickly as the tear appeared, the girl slapped it away with her shirt sleeve, and she said with determination, "Let's get these dishes done. Baby Girl wants a story."

Chapter 25

Charles and Sarah were having a late breakfast in the dining room of the lodge. Sitting by the bay window, they looked out beyond the woods at the rolling mountains and the clear blue sky. "What a beautiful day," Sarah exclaimed. "Let's take the children somewhere today."

Charles looked down and Sarah could see a tightness in his face. "Charles? Is something wrong?"

"I was just thinking about the children. You know, we'll have to leave soon and go back to our lives, and these children …"

"I know," she said sadly. "Life is about to be turned upside down for these children. I guess that's why I was hoping to give them one really fun day."

"I guess I'm having trouble giving up on the idea of finding Abernathy," Charles said. "What I'm struggling with is the fact that even though I've been following dead ends, I've had this constant feeling that Abernathy was out there waiting to be found. I have no proof or logical explanation; it's just a vague feeling, but a feeling that I've grown to trust over the years."

"You think there's more we can do?" she asked, looking skeptical.

"I'm waiting to hear what John learned from his FBI friend. I keep thinking about the two or three workers that disappeared from Mickelson's a few years ago. Maybe Abernathy found out something and they made him disappear as well. I just don't feel comfortable leaving when I feel there's so much more to know."

"Let's call your son this morning," Sarah suggested. "Maybe John's heard from his FBI friend."

"But John said he'd call when he learned something" Looking at Sarah, he added, "I keep wondering if I should go back up to Mickelson."

"Oh, good idea," she responded sarcastically. "And they're going to say, 'yes, we killed him and buried the body.' Charles, you can't put yourself in that kind of danger. You don't know how I felt when ..." her voice cracked, and she looked away until she was able to compose herself. "When I thought something had happened to you ..."

"Sarah, I do know, because I know how I'd feel if I thought I was losing you. Okay, you're probably right about me going up there. I'll wait to hear from John."

They picked at the rest of their breakfast, but had both lost their appetite. "Show me your nature path," Charles said as they were leaving the dining room.

"Oh! That sounds like fun. I'll show you the overlook where I placed my calls to you. It's beautiful up there."

Hand in hand, they walked up the gravel path and out to the overlook. "See over there by that stream? That's the children's house. Ricky comes up here by crossing that gorge and climbing this steep rocky wall below us."

Charles cautiously leaned out over the precipice and looked down. "That's so dangerous, Sarah. So dangerous. These children need supervision."

Sarah smiled, realizing these self-sufficient children could survive a lot longer than she or Charles could if they were left to survive on their own in the mountains.

"Let's sit down on that boulder over there and call John," Sarah suggested again. "He's a busy lawyer, and he just might have forgotten."

"Shouldn't we wait until later in the day?"

"It's early there right now, and he probably hasn't gone into the office yet. Let's just try, okay?" She was eager to get closure on the Mickelson issues, fearing that Charles would head back up there alone.

"Okay." Charles sat down and Sarah sat next to him. After he dialed, he slipped his arm around her and gently pulled her close to his side. From a distance, one would mistake them for young lovers on their honeymoon.

"John, it's Dad."

"Great timing," John responded cheerfully. "I heard from Seymour late last night and started to call you, but I remembered it was the middle of the night on the east coast."

Eager to hear what Seymour had to say, he asked, "So, what did you learn?"

"Okay, Dad. Here's what he had to say. What you heard was partly right; it was just way out of date. A few years ago, the Russian Mafia got their claws into Mickelson's Mining. The elder Mickelson, Joseph Mickelson, Sr., ended up dead and the FBI got involved. Over a period of two or three months several arrests were made, and several key witnesses were moved into the witness protection program.

As far as the other workers were concerned, those people simply disappeared. From there, the rumor mill took over. Mickelson's been clean since then, as far as we know. There's some pretty close scrutiny going on at the state and local levels. Seymour doesn't think Mickelson's had anything to do with your friend's disappearance, and after hearing the whole story, I agree."

"Yeah. From what you've said, I'd have to admit that I agree too. With all that monitoring, they'd be fools to pull anything illegal."

"So, Pop. How's it going up there? Do you have any other leads?"

"Not a one. I chased my tail for several days up in West Virginia and got nowhere. I'm back at the lodge now," he added, deciding not to mention the layover at the hospital. "And we're trying to decide whether to give up and get these kids placed with relatives or keep looking."

"How long has the man been gone?" John asked.

"It's been almost two months now since he was reportedly seen leaving the work site."

"And, of course, you've checked to make sure he's not in jail or hospitalized."

"I did that right away after I arrived. ..." Charles hesitated a moment and looked over at Sarah. "I checked the large hospitals, but now that you mention it, I was asking about a Richard Abernathy. I never thought to ask about a John Doe."

"Why would he be a John Doe? You said he drove away; he would have had his identification with him, wouldn't he?" John asked.

"As a matter of fact, Mickelson's had his wallet with all his identification. They said he left in a hurry and left his wallet in his locker. What if …?" he glanced at Sarah and saw a look of despair, and he was sorry he had the phone on speaker. If Abernathy had been listed as a John Doe, that would most likely mean he was dead.

* * * * *

Later that afternoon as they were driving up to the Abernathy home, Charles suddenly said, "I think you're right."

"About what?" she asked.

"About taking the children out for the rest of the day. Where could we take them?"

"Well, you have your phone with instant access to the internet, and I still don't know how that can possibly work," she added as an aside. "Anyway, see if there are any amusement parks around. That would be fun for the children, and Baby Girl and I could ride on one of the calmer rides, like a carousel, if they even have those anymore."

"Good idea. You go on in and make sure the kids have had lunch, and I'll stay out here and find something fun to do."

After a couple of searches, he suddenly said aloud, "That's it!"

"What's it?" a young voice asked. When he looked down, he saw Tommy looking up at him and carrying a small kitten.

"Where'd you find that?" Charles asked petting the small head which pushed into his hand with a force he couldn't believe possible from such a small creature.

"Under the house."

"Did you see the mother cat under there?"

"Nope. He was alone and shivering. I wanna keep him inside. He'll freeze out here."

"Let's go inside and talk to Addie May about it."

When they walked in the door, Addie May handed Tommy a box that had been lined with fabric scraps. "Now take him into the kitchen and put him near the stove where he'll be warm."

Tommy looked up at Charles and smiled before going over to Addie May and hugging her. "Thanks," he said lovingly.

"What was that all about?" Sarah whispered to Charles.

"Tell you later," he responded with a smile. "Now, let me tell you what I found.

The children piled into the car, all talking at once with excitement. "What's a moosement park?" Baby Girl kept asking. Addie May tried to explain it to her, but the concept was way above the child's head.

Finally Ricky spoke up and simply said, "Just wait and see." The little girl accepted this word from her big brother and sat quietly until they arrived.

For the next few hours, the two boys rode together on trains and airplanes and seats that swung out over the heads of the onlookers. Sarah found a merry-go-round, and she and Addie May stood on opposite sides of the horse Baby Girl had picked out and held onto her as she went up and down with the music. Sarah had to laugh at the look on the child's face, somewhere between ecstasy and terror. They played games, and the boys won several plastic coffee mugs at the shooting gallery after Charles gave them a quick lesson.

"Here, you can have this," Tommy said, handing his winnings to Sarah.

Ricky watched, but hesitated and finally said, "Is it okay if I save mine for Dad?"

"Of course," she said, finally giving into her impulse to hug him. She was surprised that he returned the hug before squaring up his shoulders and walking away.

Charles took care of the three younger children while Sarah and Addie May went on the Ferris wheel. The young girl's eyes sparkled and she squealed the first time they cleared the top and started down the other side. "I love this," she told Sarah once she settled into the rhythm of the ride.

"Where do you think they got to?" Addie May asked once they were back on the ground.

"They'll find us. Let's get an ice cream cone." Moments later, Charles came running up and put Baby Girl into Sarah's arms. "What's happening?" Sarah asked.

"The boys and I have plans," and he ran off with the boys in tow.

A few minutes later, she and Addie May heard screams from the direction of the roller coaster and, sure enough, there were both the boys and Charles squeezed into the front seat as it careened up and down the track. Charles waved when they got off the ride but, instead of joining her, the three ran and got at the end of the line to do it again.

The girls sat eating their cones and watched the boys take two more turns on the roller coaster.

On their way home, they stopped at a fast-food restaurant for a dinner of burgers, fries, and milk shakes for everyone but Charles. He had a grilled chicken sandwich and hardly

grumbled about it. He told Sarah later he hadn't had that much fun since his own boys were young.

Sarah and Charles stayed until the three younger Abernathy children were in bed. Sarah kissed Addie May goodbye, and they headed back to their temporary home on the top of the ridge.

Chapter 26

"You have a message," the night clerk announced as they entered the lodge. Charles took the note and frowned when he read the name.

"What is it?" Sarah asked.

"Stevenson called. Marshall Stevenson." He looked bewildered.

"That name sounds familiar, but I don't remember. Who is he?" Sarah asked.

"He's the foreman at Mickelson."

"Calling you? Why?"

"I have no idea. Maybe he's learned something?" he speculated.

"Or maybe he found out that you had the FBI sniffing around?" Sarah suggested.

"That's a thought. I'll call and see."

As it turned out, the number was not Stevenson's personal cell but rather the worksite. Charles left his cell phone number on the machine.

"That's strange. I don't know why he called the lodge. I gave him my cell phone number when I was up there. I guess I gave him this number too." He pulled his cell phone out of

his pocket and realized it was turned off. "Ah. I turned this thing off when we were on the roller coaster. I remember now that it rang and I could see you down there watching and since it wasn't you calling me, I just switched it off. I forgot all about it." Turning it on, he remarked. "Yep. It's the same number." He clicked the speaker on and played the message."

"Parker, I need to speak with you right away. If you don't get this before 6:00 tonight, call me in the morning. I have some information for you."

Charles turned the television on and said, "Let's just relax tonight. In the morning I'll call Stevenson, and then I want to start calling the hospitals again."

"I'll sit and watch with you, but I need to finish hemming the binding on the children's quilt. I promised I'd do that for them." She had attached it the previous day using Addie May's machine but still had the hand sewing to do. Pulling out the quilt and her sewing box, she sat next to Charles by the window. They kept the shades open, and the moon cast a shimmering light over the tree tops. Charles scanned through the movie titles.

"Remember," she said playfully, "you still owe me a chick flick."

* * * * *

"Stevenson," the man bellowed trying to speak over the background noise. "Hey guys, keep it down. I'm trying to talk." Turning back to the phone, he continued, "Sorry."

"Good morning, Marshall. It's Charles Parker returning your call."

"Good. I wanted to tell you about this call I got from Bryston yesterday."

"Bryston?"

"Bryston, Ohio. That's our home office. Anyway, some hospital in Virginia was calling them about a patient they had with no identification. They said they had part of a pay stub that had the company name on it. It had our site code on it, and the bosses were calling to find out if we knew who it might be. I thought it might be Abernathy."

"And they are just now finding it?"

"You'd have to ask them about that. Do you want the number?"

"Of course, I do. This is the most promising lead we've had. And they said he was in the hospital? Not the morgue?"

"It was the hospital that called, so I'd guess he's a patient. I don't know why he wouldn't just tell them his name though. The whole thing sounds fishy."

"Fishy is better than nothing. I'll give the hospital a call and check this out. Thanks for calling, Marshall. You know, he's got a family down here and we're all hoping …"

"Yep. And if you find the guy and he's okay, tell him he has a job here if he wants it. Best worker I ever had."

"I'm driving up to Virginia to check this out," Charles said after filling Sarah in about his conversations with the Mickelson foreman and the social worker at the medical center.

They were both excited about the possibility of finding Abernathy, but on the other hand, they were reticent since, if it was in fact him, he obviously couldn't identify himself. "Do you want to go with me?"

"How far is it?"

"It's a little over three hours," he responded. "I want to get some breakfast first and take off right after that."

"Okay, I'd like to go with you." She looked over at the quilt she had finished hemming the night before.

"Do you want to go by the house before we leave?" he asked.

"No. I'm afraid Addie May would sense that something was happening and I don't want to disappoint her. I think it's unlikely we're going to get good news."

* * * * *

"We're here to see Katherine Lathrop."

"Lathrop? Is she a patient here?" the volunteer receptionist asked.

"No, she's the hospital social worker."

"Oh, yes. I'll ring her phone." After a short delay, she said, "Ms. Lathrop will be right out. Just have a seat."

"I'm so glad to see you folks," the young woman said as she came out into the lobby. "We've had this gentleman with us for many weeks and we've had no idea how to reach his family. Are you family?"

Charles stood to shake her hand and said, "We represent the man's family, but we don't even know if this is the man we're searching for. Why aren't you able to get this man's name from him?"

"He's in a coma following a terrible accident up in the mountains. He was found unconscious in a ravine, and no one knows just how long he was there." Hesitating a moment, she asked, "You say you represent his family?"

"I'm sorry," Sarah suddenly spoke up. "I'm Sarah Parker and this is my husband, Detective Charles Parker. We've been asked by the family to assist in the search for a Richard Abernathy. We're hoping your unidentified patient might be Mr. Abernathy."

Charles looked at her somewhat surprised that she was slightly twisting the truth. She later whispered to him, "You know how fearful these places are about sharing medical information with the wrong person."

He then reached into his breast pocket and pulled out the picture of Abernathy. He now had a blowup of the driver's license picture obtained for him by Marvin, the deputy in Beaver Creek.

"Yes, that's our Mr. John Doe," the young woman responded with excitement. "I thought we'd never identify him. What's his name again?"

"Abernathy. Richard Abernathy."

"You say he's in a coma?" Sarah said. "That sounds very serious."

"Let's go back to my office where we can speak freely." Sarah and Charles followed Ms. Lathrop down the hall to an area marked Social Services. They took seats in her office and she offered them coffee. Sarah declined, but Charles said he'd have a cup.

"Let's see how your coffee compares to the sludge we serve in the department," Charles said, continuing with Sarah's deception.

"From what our local cops tell me, ours is not much better." She noted that Sarah Parker had remained solemn since asking about Abernathy's condition, and she wanted to offer some relief. "I just spoke with the doctor this morning and they are hopeful. His vitals have been good for the past few weeks. His wounds have healed, but, of course, without exercise, he's experiencing some atrophy. The nurses try to help, but there's only so much they can do."

"I have one question," Charles said. "If you folks had this pay stub, why did it take two months to notify the company?"

The social worker looked offended. "I'm the one that called that company, Detective Parker, and I'm extremely proud of the work I did. This is what I had to work with," she said as she reached into her desk drawer and pulled out a scrap of paper which appeared to be part of a torn pay stub. She handed it to Charles.

"MICK ..." was printed in the upper left-hand corner of the stub. There was a diagonal tear that ran from the K down to the bottom right-hand side of the stub which removed the rest of the company name and much of the information below it. The words "Employee No." appeared at the middle of the stub, but the tear had removed the number. At the bottom of the stub "Site No. 900" appeared along with part of a letter which could be a B.

"This was found inside the wreckage and was brought along with him when he was admitted. I've talked with dozens of companies beginning with 'Mick', asking them if they have a site number that begins with nine-zero-zero and whether they had a missing worker." Still looking defensive, she continued, "It wasn't until two days ago that I got a positive response. I was ecstatic when I finally spoke with Mickelson's and even more so when you called."

"I'm sorry, Ms. Lathrop. I didn't mean to be discourteous. I've had family members come into the station accusing me of doing nothing when I've been working my butt off. I know how you feel and I'm sincerely sorry."

The social worker nodded her acceptance of his apology and said. "Would you like to see him now?"

* * * * *

"And you are?" the doctor said, turning away from his patient as the three entered.

"How do you do," Sarah responded quickly before Charles could speak. "I'm Sarah Parker and I represent this man's sister-in-law who lives in Portland, Oregon." As she spoke, she handed him a sheet of paper. "Here is her name and number if you need to speak with her. We're hoping to get information about Richard's condition so we can plan for the children," she continued in a very take-charge tone.

That's my wife, Charles thought proudly as he saw how quickly she came up with a cover story. *Not that it isn't all true*, he thought, *but she cleverly planted her story before the doctor had a chance to challenge her right to patient information.*

"I'm glad you're here," the doctor responded, turning back to the patient. "We've been concerned about notifying the family of this gentleman. By the way, I'm Doctor Feldman," he said turning to Charles and extending his hand.

"I'm Charles Parker," he said simply, seeing that his wife was taking the lead on this one.

"Can you tell us what happened?" Sarah asked.

"Mr. Abernathy was found unconscious and lying near his car down in a ravine just south of Bristol City. There are dangerous curves in that area, and we assumed that he just lost control of the car.

"How long was he down there?" Sarah asked.

"No one knows. The police reported that the car was cold and it could have been there for a couple of days. He was obviously taking a short cut over the mountains. Should've stuck to the interstate," he added as he checked the man's feet for responses. "See that?" he said proudly.

"What?" Sarah asked.

"He's beginning to respond to touch. The nurse said he opened his eyes for a moment when she was exercising his arms. It's not like it is in the movies, you know. Folks don't hop up from a coma and begin to sing an aria from *La Bohème*. It's a slow, step-by-step process. As for Mr. Abernathy, his vitals have been strong for weeks now. His EEG shows adequate brain activity. He's responding to touch and we've seen some indication that he's aware of our presence. This man will be back with us soon."

"And he'll be fine?"

"I can't say that at this time, although he may well return to his previous level of functioning. He'll need physical and possibly vocational therapy. It just depends."

"What caused the coma?" Charles asked.

"Well, a combination of factors. He had a severe head injury affecting the cerebral cortex; he also suffered hypothermia and excessive blood loss. He's actually a lucky fellow considering what could have been. It's just a good thing someone spotted the car down there when they did."

The doctor excused himself, leaving Sarah and Charles with this stranger who had been in their hearts and prayers for the past weeks. "I think we need to make absolutely certain," Charles said. He took out his phone and took a picture close to the man's face. Sarah thought she saw Richard flinch when the light flashed.

Charles dialed Jack Slocum's number and told him where they were. "I have another picture for you," and he hit the send button and put the phone on speaker so Sarah could listen.

"That's our guy," Jack Slocum cried out. "That's him. Oh, man, you did it. Mary Beth, Cody, come see this picture." Charles could hear the sounds of excitement in the background. "Do his kids know?" Slocum asked.

"Not yet," Charles responded, "but let us tell them, okay? We still don't know how long it will be before he's home and, to tell you the truth, no one knows what condition he'll be in. There was a serious head injury."

"Don't worry. When he gets home, I've got the perfect job for him here in the lodge. No more driving cross country to slice the top off mountains."

At that moment, Richard Abernathy opened his eyes and looked directly at Sarah. As he closed them again, Sarah saw a tear leak down the side of his face. She reached for a tissue and wiped it away. "Would you go get me a cup of coffee, Charles? I'd like to sit here with Richard. I have a few things to tell him." Not knowing whether he could hear her or not, she told him all the things the children had been doing, about the beef stew Addie May had made all alone, about Baby Girl who wants to be named Clara like her mother, and about their trip to the amusement park. She described the boys on the roller coaster and Baby Girl riding up and down on the carousel.

She didn't know if he was able to hear her, but in her heart she felt him smile.

Chapter 27

"Sophie, we've got news!" Sarah said excitedly when Sophie answered the phone. It had been several days since they returned from Virginia, but Sarah had been reluctant to tell anyone about Richard's condition. She didn't want to get her own hopes up and especially not the children's. But word from the doctor had been encouraging and she wanted to talk to Sophie about it. "We found the children's father."

"Alive?" Sophie asked tentatively.

"Alive, yes, but in a coma. The doctor is optimistic though." She went on to catch Sophie up on all the details. "Once he regains consciousness, there'll be months of physical and vocational therapy. ..."

"And you'll be staying down there?" Sophie interrupted.

"No Sophie, Charles and I agree it's time for the family to take over. I'm going to call the aunt in the morning and suggest she either come here and stay with the children or come get them and take them to Portland until the father has recuperated. As much as I hate leaving the children, it's time for Charles and me to get back to our lives."

"From what you told me," Sophie responded tentatively, "it sounds like this aunt is living the good life in Portland. Are you sure she can survive in that primitive mountain cabin?"

"You're forgetting something, Sophie. Rosalie grew up in that house!"

"You're right, I had forgotten that. So what happens next?"

"We're going to talk to the doctor tomorrow to find out just what's in store for Richard. Charles thinks they might be able to move him down here to Gatlinburg for his therapy. That way the children could visit him. It would probably help with his recovery."

"But," Sophie interrupted, "he isn't even out of the coma at this point."

"That's true, but the doctor thinks it's just a matter of time. He's totally recovered from the accident, has strong vital signs, and several times he's actually opened his eyes for a few moments."

"Really?" Sophie responded with surprise.

"And when we were in his room and talking about him coming home," Sarah continued, "a tear ran down the side of his face. He could hear us!" she added with restrained enthusiasm. "I just know he was listening!"

Sarah was speaking with Sophie on the lodge telephone in their room, and she suddenly heard her cell phone ringing. "Charles, can you get my cell?"

"Got it, sweetie, … Hello?"

He remained quiet as he listened to the caller, and then began to smile. He looked over at Sarah and winked.

"I've got to go Sophie. I'll call you tomorrow and let you know what's happening." As she hung up, she turned to Charles and raised her eyebrows. "Good news?" she asked in a whisper. He gestured for her to wait just a moment as he was saying goodbye to the caller.

"Richard is among the living," he announced with a tremendous grin. "He opened his eyes this morning while the doctor was examining him and said a few words." Charles had an impish look on his face.

"What?" Sarah asked.

"He wants to see the kind lady."

"The kind lady?" she repeated, looking confused.

"You, my dear. He's asking for the kind lady who told him stories about his children."

"Oh, Charles!" she exclaimed as she rushed into his arms. He held her close and whispered, "Those kids are going to have their father back."

"Let's call Rosalie right away," she said, eager to set their plan in motion. As much as she loved the children, she was ready to get back to her life in Cunningham Village. She missed her friends, her home, and especially her dog, Barney. "I'll bet he thinks we've deserted him."

"Who?" Charles responding, not being privy to her thoughts.

"Barney, of course," she responded as she picked up the phone. "Let's call Rosalie, and then let's go tell the children everything that's happened."

"Can we slip breakfast in there somewhere? I'm starved!"

* * * * *

Ricky threw his arms around Sarah's neck and squealed with joy. "I knew you could do it," he was saying. "I knew it when I heard you talking on your phone up on the cliff."

"You did?" Sarah said pulling back enough to see into his eyes. "What did you know?"

"You were talking to a friend about some kind of problem and you sounded wise and caring. That's when I decided to ask you to help us."

She pulled him close again and whispered, "I'm glad you did."

Baby Girl, now called Clara by her siblings, was running in circles singing "Daddy, daddy, daddy home." She was holding the ragdoll Sarah had brought her.

Addie May had told Sarah that the doll hadn't been out of Clara's arms since the day she got it. "She's named it Miss Sarah," Addie May had said.

Sarah looked at Addie May who had her arms around Tommy and was wiping tears from his face. "It's been hardest for Tommy," she said to Sarah later. "He and dad were together all the time. He was barely four when Mama died and he latched onto our father. It's been hardest for him, I'd say …" She looked away and Sarah knew she was fighting tears of relief.

"I would guess it's been hardest on you, my dear. You've carried the adult burden of raising a family, but relief is on its way."

"What do you mean? You said daddy would be in the hospital for many months."

"Let's sit down and have a cup of coffee," Sarah responded. "I have more news for you." Sarah poured two cups of coffee, a full cup for herself and a half-cup for Addie May which she then filled to the brim with warmed milk and a generous helping of sugar, just the way Addie May liked it.

"This is just the way Mama used to make it for me," she said as she took a sip.

"I know," Sarah said, remembering the night she and the young girl sat on the porch sharing memories from times past.

"So, what is the rest of the news?" Addie May asked, eager to hear what was in store for her family.

"Okay, first of all, we talked to the doctor and he said there's no reason your father needs to stay so far away. They are going to arrange to transport him to Gatlinburg for his rehabilitation. That way you kids can visit him."

Addie May looked reluctant. "How will we get there?" she asked. Sarah had already explained that she and Charles would be leaving soon.

"That's the other news. Your Aunt Rosie is on her way. She's going to stay here with you as long as it takes for your father to get home."

Addie May sat quietly and tears began to seep from her eyes. At first, Sarah thought she was unhappy, but she saw the smallest twitch of the girl's cheek as a smile broke through the tears. "Our Aunt Rosie is coming here?" she asked, hardly able to believe what she was hearing.

"She said for me to tell you that your mother always called her Rosie, and she'd love for you to call her Aunt Rosie."

"Aunt Rosie," Addie May repeated with a smile. She hopped up from the table and ran into the living room where the children were watching the small television set Charles had installed for them. "Guess what?" she announced.

"We have an Aunt Rosie and she's coming to stay with us until Papa comes home!" All four kids were whooping and bouncing around the room in time with a cartoon featuring dancing dinosaurs.

After a dinner of fried chicken and all the trimmings, Sarah and Addie May did the dishes and talked about the future. Sarah explained what little she knew about Richard's therapy and assured her he was going to be fine. "Charles and I both talked to the doctor this morning. Your dad has already been out of bed and is doing remarkably well." She didn't go on to explain the details to Addie May, but the doctor had said that the coma had served to give Richard time for his body to heal. He said Richard may experience some deficits but all that would be addressed in rehab. "Your Aunt Rosie will handle everything once she gets here, and you'll be able to visit your dad."

"When will she be here?" Addie May asked.

"Coby is picking her up in Knoxville tomorrow afternoon. I'll come over in the morning, and we'll fix up a room for her and get the housework caught up."

"Good," she responded, "and maybe I can make a big pot of stew for dinner."

"Perfect."

Addie May turned to Sarah and put her arms around her. "Thank you for everything, Miss Sarah. God sent you to us. I prayed every night for help."

"You're very welcome, Addie May. I'm glad I could be here, but you've done a wonderful job with your brothers and the baby. I'm just glad help is on the way. It's time for you to be one of the kids yourself."

Addie May laughed. "I haven't been a kid since Mama died."

"Well, then, it's about time."

On the way back to the lodge, Sarah reached for Charles' hand and said, "What would you think of making reservations for us to fly home in a few days?"

Chapter 28

"Flight 922 now boarding, Gate 25B."

"Come on, honey," Charles called. "Let's get in line." As they approached the gate, Sarah's cell phone rang.

"Better turn that off," Charles reminded her.

"But it's Sophie." Sarah stepped out of line and put the phone to her ear. "Hello?"

"Hi, kiddo. I have something I want to read to you."

"Make it fast, Sophie. We're about to board the plane."

"Okay. Well, remember that SUV that Higginbottom left parked in front of my house?"

"Yes," Sarah responded, holding a finger up indicating that Charles should wait a minute."

"Well, I received a certified letter today from Las Vegas."

"What does it say?" she asked, beginning to get curious but seeing that Charles was becoming impatient.

"Hurry," he called to her trying to save her place in line.

"Last call for Flight 922, Gate 25B."

"Sophie …?"

"Honey, are you coming, or should I get out of line?" Charles' voice had taken on an edgy tone.

Sarah signaled for him to stay in line. "Just let a few people go ahead of you," she called to him. To Sophie she said, "Hurry, Sophie. We're going to miss our flight."

"Okay," Sophie responded and she began to read.

I know I haven't treated you right,
But I was thinking just last night,
That maybe you'd think better of me,
If I were to give you my SUV.
I've signed the title over to you.
That makes me feel a little less blue.
I hope you'll accept this token from me,
And by the way, enclosed is the key.

"Good grief, Sophie. That's quite a gift. Does this mean you might take him back?" Sarah asked reluctantly.

"Absolutely not," Sophie announced emphatically. "But I fully intend to make the most of that fancy SUV in my driveway.

Sarah and Charles boarded the plane with Charles shaking his head as Sarah recapped Sophie's call. "What are these big plans of hers?" he asked.

"She said she hasn't figured it out yet, but we'll be the first to know when she does."

"There's no telling what that feisty friend of yours will come up with," Charles said with a chuckle.

They sat holding hands as the plane took off for home.

*See full
quilt on
back cover.*

MOON OVER THE MOUNTAIN

At a quilt retreat in the Appalachians,
Sarah relaxed on the porch enjoying the view
of the harvest moon and the mountains. This 21″ × 19″
wall hanging commemorates her time there.

MATERIALS

Moon: ⅜ yard

Mountain: Strips of 5–7 assorted fabrics,
2″–3½″ wide × 5″–19″ long

Background: ⅝ yard

Backing: ⅔ yard

Batting: 24″ × 22″

Binding: ¼ yard

Fusible stabilizer: Such as Stabili-TEE Fusible Interfacing
by C&T Publishing: 21″ × 19″

Foundation paper: Such as Carol Doak's
Legal-Size Foundation Paper by C&T Publishing:
Cut 1 square 13½″ × 13½″.

Paper-backed fusible web: 17″ wide, ¾ yard

PROJECT

Project Instructions

Seam allowances are ¼". Follow package instructions for fusibles.

MAKE THE BACKGROUND, MOON, AND MOUNTAIN

Tip || Trace around a dinner plate to get the circle for the moon.

1. Cut the background 21" × 19". Iron stabilizer to the wrong side of the background.

2. Cut the web 11" × 11" and fuse to the wrong side of the moon fabric. Draw a circle 10½" in diameter on the paper side of the fusible web. Cut on the drawn line.

3. Join 2 pieces of foundation paper with masking tape. Cut a square 13½" × 13½", and then cut it on the diagonal to get 2 triangles. (You'll use only 1 triangle.)

4. Place a strip of mountain fabric, right side up, across the long edge of a foundation-paper triangle, leaving a slight overhang. Place a second strip, right side down, on the first strip, aligning the long edges. Sew together through the strips and the paper. Press. Continue adding strips until the triangle is completely covered.

Foundation paper under the mountain strips

6. Trim the mountain even with the triangle paper. Remove the paper. Fuse the web to the wrong side of the mountain.

APPLIQUÉ AND ASSEMBLE THE QUILT

1. Fuse the moon to the stabilized background, centering it 2½″ from the top edge. Sew around the moon's edges with a narrow zigzag stitch to secure.

2. Fuse the mountain to the background, centering it 2″ from the bottom edge. Sew around the mountain's edges with a narrow zigzag stitch to secure.

3. Layer the appliquéd top with batting and backing. Quilt and bind as desired.

PROJECT

Turn the page for a preview --------------------------→
of the next book in A Quilting Cozy series.

2nd edition includes instructions to make the featured quilt

The Rescue Quilt

a quilting cozy

Carol Dean Jones

Preview of
The Rescue Quilt

Sarah chose a table by the window so she could watch for Sophie. A red SUV pulled up in front of the café, displaying a sign identifying it as the Pup Mobile. Sarah sighed and looked at her watch, wondering what was keeping Sophie. The waitress glanced at the vehicle as she waited for Sarah's order. "I'll just have coffee until my friend gets here," Sarah said as she turned to take another look outside. "Wait," she said with astonishment. "That's my friend getting out of that SUV, but why …?"

Moments later, Sophie entered the café and hurried to the table as quickly as her new titanium knee would permit. "Hi, toots," she announced, using the annoying pet term she learned from her ex-fiancé, Cornelius Higginbottom.

"Don't *toots* me," Sarah teased, "and what's with the sign painted on your new SUV?"

"Actually, that's a magnetized sheet that I just slap on when I'm working."

"Working?" Sarah responded with surprise. She wondered if she'd missed an important chapter in Sophie's life while she was away at her quilting retreat in Tennessee. "Sit down and tell me what's going on."

Sophie unwrapped the hot-pink scarf she had twisted around her neck, pulled off her matching cap and gloves, and removed her coat to reveal her new chartreuse running suit. "Do you like it?" she asked as she slowly spun her short, rotund body around, giving Sarah a view from all angles.

"It's adorable, Sophie. Now, what do you mean *working*?"

Sophie signaled for the waitress and took a few minutes perusing the menu. "How are your bacon burgers?" she asked.

Before the waitress could respond, Sarah said, "I would guess they're the same as the ones you've had every week for the past ten years. Order and tell me what's going on."

"You're getting really pushy in your old age," Sophie grumbled. She ordered the burger and added fried onions and cheddar cheese as she always did.

After sitting and looking at one another for a moment, Sarah raised both eyebrows and said, "So?"

"Okay. You're not going to rest until I tell you the whole story, so here goes. My friend Maria called while you were away and asked me to give her a hand. You know her, right?"

"Yes, I know her from classes at the community center. And doesn't she have that granddaughter who was written up in the local paper last month?"

"That's right. Kelly is her granddaughter, and Maria is a volunteer driver for a local animal rescue organization."

"And the Pup Mobile?" Sarah asked.

"I'm getting there. Be patient." Sophie took a sip of her coffee and added two more sugar packets. "Okay. A few weeks ago," she continued, "Kelly asked her grandmother to pick up a little dog from the shelter and drive him out to her farm. Kelly was going to foster him until his forever family got settled in their new home."

"And Maria asked you to go with her?" Sarah interjected, attempting to move the story along.

"Actually, she asked me to drive. Her car was in the shop."

"Ah. And you did?"

"I did. We picked this little fellow up and put his crate in the back seat of my SUV. He was a cute little guy, with long hair, a squished-up face, and a cute little button nose. His name was Buddy." Sarah smiled, enjoying this rarely seen side of Sophie. "Anyway," Sophie continued, "as we were driving, Maria told me about her volunteer job providing transportation for this group called Sheila's Shuttle."

"Who do they transport, exactly?" Sarah asked, still not clear how the story fit together.

"Maria drives dogs mostly, sometimes cats. She takes them to no-kill shelters and foster homes, and sometimes she takes newly adopted ones to their forever homes. Other times she just takes them to meet the next driver along the way to their final destination. She said there's a whole network of volunteers who provide rescue transportation all over the country."

"Hmm," Sarah responded thoughtfully. "Are you thinking of adopting one of these dogs?"

"You know better than that. I can't take care of a dog."

"You certainly could if ..."

"Sarah, do you want to hear my story or not?"

"Sorry, Sophie. Please finish your story. "

"Okay, here's what I'm doing ..."

At that moment, Sophie's cell phone rang. She pulled it out of her pocket and looked at the display. "It's Timmy," she announced excitedly. Timmy was her son who had been working on the Alaska pipeline for the past thirty-five years. "Timmy, I'm so glad you called," Sarah heard her say. "Have you turned in your retirement papers yet?"

Sarah stood up and walked to the counter to get a newspaper and to give her friend some privacy. Sophie, older than Sarah by a few years, wasn't in the best physical condition, and Sarah wondered what she was planning. She was beginning to realize that it probably had something to do with rescuing animals. She hoped so. Sophie was a warm and caring person who tried to hide behind a rough exterior, but Sarah knew she had a tender heart.

Sarah met Sophie the day she moved into Cunningham Village; they had become close friends, with Sophie helping Sarah make the difficult transition into a retirement community. At that time, they lived across the street from each other, but Sarah had since moved into a house in a newer section of the village that catered to couples. And after twenty years as a widow, Sarah was now officially part of a couple. On a snowy New Year's Eve, she had married Charles, a retired policeman whom she adored and who adored her.

"I'm so excited, Timmy," Sarah heard her friend squeal from her table as she was saying goodbye to her son. Sophie signaled for Sarah to return to the table and announced with excitement, "He turned in his retirement papers, and he'll be home in a couple of months. I can hardly believe it," she added looking relieved. "I was beginning to think he'd never leave Alaska."

"Did he say anything about his plans once he gets here?" Sarah asked, wondering if he planned to make his home in Middletown.

"Only that he can't wait to see Martha," she responded with a mischievous grin. Martha was Sarah's forty-five-year-old daughter. She and Tim had met the previous year when he was visiting his mother, and they had instantly hit it off. Sophie and Sarah kidded about becoming mutual mothers-in-law, but neither Tim nor Martha would discuss the possibility.

"So," Sarah began. "Do you think you can finally tell me what you and your decorated SUV are up to?"

* * * * *

"So she's going to be driving rescued dogs?" Charles repeated with a chuckle. "Your outrageous friend is full of surprises." He shook his head in mock skepticism, but his eyes were twinkling with amusement.

"Well, here's what she told me," Sarah began. "Her friend Maria, who has been volunteering as a driver for a local rescue organization, asked Sophie to drive her on a couple of her assignments while her car was in the shop."

"Do we know this Maria?"

"Yes. Maria Wilcox. You met her at the pool last month. She was swimming laps next to you during my water aerobics class. She has a very special granddaughter. This young woman, I believe her name is Kelly, has a farm outside of town. A few years ago she took in a goat that had come to the attention of Animal Control. He'd been neglected and abused for years and was practically dead. She nursed him back to health and gave him a loving home."

"I read an article about her a few months ago," Charles responded. "She's turned her farm into a foster home for abandoned or abused animals of all kinds. She's got a few horses, a miniature pony, two goats, and lots of dogs and cats. The reporter was asking for donations for food and medical care. I was thinking about sending them a check."

"Yes," Sarah responded, "I read that article, and I think we should. Anyway, back to Sophie's story. She drove Maria for a week or so until Maria's car was repaired, and she really enjoyed it. So when Maria told her she wanted to take a couple of months off and visit her sister Caterina in Italy, Sophie volunteered to take the runs for her while she was away. She's been doing it for a couple of weeks now, and she loves it. She even has a fancy sign on the side of her SUV identifying herself as the Pup Mobile."

"No cats?"

"No. She's allergic."

"Won't this involve lots of driving? That article said the animals come from all over the country."

"She'll be part of a network. I don't think they have to drive more than a couple hours. The volunteers tag team when the locations are far apart."

"I've got to admire Sophie for taking this on at her age," Charles responded thoughtfully.

"Timothy called today, and he's turned in his retirement papers and will be back here in a few months. I'm sure he'll help his mom if she needs him."

Charles laughed. "If she can get him away from your daughter. Martha told me that she and Tim have been on the phone almost every night since she visited him in Alaska. I think we'll be hearing wedding bells before long."

"We'll see." Sarah responded with a trace of hesitation in her voice. Charles looked at her inquisitively but didn't ask if she had reservations.

"Anyway," Sarah continued, ignoring his questioning look, "Sophie wants me to ride along with her tomorrow. She's taking two young dogs to the greyhound rescue in Hamilton. We'll be gone for several hours. I want to stop at the mall, and if I know Sophie, she'll want to work in lunch somewhere along the way."

"That works for me," Charles responded. "I'm going to be working tomorrow. I'd like to talk to a few of the neighbors around that crime scene over on the east side. Sometimes fresh eyes can spot an inconsistency. It doesn't seem logical that no one saw or heard anything considering …" Charles stopped in the middle of the sentence. He rarely discussed the details of the cases he worked on, and this one involved senior citizens and was particularly grizzly. *There's lots of depravity out there, and my lovely wife doesn't need those pictures in her head*, he told himself.

Charles, retired from Middletown Police Department, had been helping his old lieutenant from time to time. Primarily, he just knocked on doors and looked for possible leads, which he'd then pass on. He missed police work and enjoyed the feeling of being included, even at this minimal level.

"There's something I wanted to ask you," Charles began somewhat awkwardly.

"What is it?" Sarah responded, sitting down at the kitchen table with him.

"Well, I was trying to surprise you with an anniversary party at the community center."

"Oh, Charles, what a sweet thing to do …"

"… but I'm having trouble pulling all the pieces together," he continued. "I'm not much good at this kind of thing, so …"

"So, you'd like me to help with the planning?"

"Actually, I'd like for you to take over. I've made a real mess of it," he admitted, hanging his head in exaggerated embarrassment. "Please?"

Sarah laughed. "Well, if it's not too late to change what plans you've already made, I'd really like to have it right here at home."

"Great!" Charles responded, looking relieved. "You've solved one of the problems already. The center was already booked for New Year's Eve, and I had a caterer all set up with no place to cater."

Sarah laughed as she stood to wrap her arms around her very thoughtful husband. "Well that's solved. Bring me your invitation list and I'll take a look at it."

"Invitation list?"

"No list?"

"No, but I've mentioned it to a few people," he responded, looking embarrassed.

"Okay, let's sit down and make a list of everything that needs to be done, and you'll tell me which of those things are already arranged. Let's start with who you might have invited." Charles came up with about ten people he remembered mentioning it to, and together they listed another ten they would like to invite. "Twenty people will fit in the house comfortably if we borrow a few folding chairs from Ruth at the quilt shop."

"She has extra chairs?"

"Yes—for her classes. But now that I think about it, we should invite her, too, and perhaps ..." *What have I gotten myself into?* Sarah asked herself as she set the list aside and poured a cup of coffee. *And I haven't even started my Christmas shopping....*

A Note
from the Author

I hope you enjoyed *Moon Over the Mountain* as much as I enjoyed writing it. This is the sixth book in the Quilting Cozy Series and is followed by *The Rescue Quilt* in which Sarah and Charles struggle to solve the mystery their friend Sophie has stumbled upon.

On page 216, I have included a preview to *The Rescue Quilt* so that you can get an idea of what our cast of characters will be involved in next.

Please let me know how you are enjoying this series. I love hearing from my readers and encourage you to contact me on my blog or send me an email.

Best wishes,

Carol Dean Jones
caroldeanjones.com
quiltingcozy@gmail.com